# TIM THE LONDON TAXI AND THE GOLDEN TEDDY BEAR

*MELISSA FRANKLIN*

ISBN-978-1-63767-147-4 (Paperback)
ISBN-978-1-63767-148-1 (eBook)

Darkness can hide many secrets, horrors even the strongest man could not handle. But some secrets fight to be told, to find justice for the victims unable to defend themselves, no matter how many dark days or years have passed.

Silhouetted against the night sky lit only by the ghost like moon stood the cold stone skeleton of a large haunting ruin.

Although crumbling it stood proud, akin to the people it once housed.

The darkness of its windows like empty eyes to its broken soul, the blackened doorway, the devil's own gateway to hell.

A heavy door slams, he turns startled, the dust lingers in the air, panic rushing through his body. Turning round and around panicked, the sound of girls laughing and soldiers barking out orders, gunshots, silence. Just the sound of his blood rushing through his head and his own heavy laboured breathing.

The air thick with dust, gun smoke and the smell of fresh blood. He gagged, his hand slapped against his mouth in case anyone heard him. He was alone amongst the rubble of what was once a home, a prison.

No birds have sung in the grounds since 1918, only the bravest or stupidest people scramble through the broken down masonry and rusted barbed wire fences once erected to keep them out, if only for their own sanity.

# INTRODUCTION

Alexander was a young loyal soldier but times were changing, innocent people were suffering under the hard regime of the Bolsheviks, his views and loyalty had slowly begun to change over time. More so in June 1918 when he returned to the family he was guarding who were under strict house arrest.

The Bolshevik Secret Police were in total control at the house, they had more control than the regular Bolshevik soldiers.

One cold afternoon he had been ordered to accompany the cook Sednev to town, having been told by his commanding officer that the boy's uncle was visiting and wanted to see his nephew, the journey would take a couple of days.

He returned alone a few days later, the house was quiet, too quiet. In the cold light of day he realised there was no bird song, as Alexander cautiously approached the building he noticed empty beer bottles lying around the grounds as if there had been a party, which considering the purpose of the house and it's tenants a party should have been the last thing happening here. As he reached the main part of the building he realised the main doors had been left open, in the distance strewn around the once beautiful grounds he noticed upturned carts left where they had turned and spades covered in dirt lay by the doorway, a doorway covered with dried out mud. It was as if everyone had left in a hurry after 'the party'. Alexander slowly entered the house, calling out as he did so. No one answered, the silence hung heavy.

His heart began to beat faster, panic and fear setting in. Every room he glanced in was in a state of total chaos but still no one seemed to be here.

He turned towards the cellar, more panic rose in his tight chest engulfing him as he noticed the door was open, the fading light of day caught the walls.... bullet ridden walls. He rested his hand against the doorway to steady himself at the realisation of impending horror of the inevitable....

"Oh my love, my beautiful love no!" Alexander crept quietly into the small room, the smell told him what had happened before he even saw the carnage, the smell of gunfire lingered in the air long enough to leave an odour familiar only to a soldier. Due to the force and amount of bullets even the plaster had been blasted off the walls in huge chunks. His fingers slowly traced the crumbling holes as he walked further into the cold room, he knew deep down in his heart that no one could survive such extreme gunfire in a space as confined as this.

Falling to his knees he sobbed into his hands that now covered his ashen face, he winced as he knelt on a stone. Motioning to flick it away he stopped as the colour caught his eye, red, ruby red set in gold. Picking it up his mind flashed back to when he gave it to Shvybz, his Shvybz, clutching it in his shaking hand he cried for his young love, knowing she and her family were gone.

He knew he couldn't stay long, it wouldn't be safe. After searching the whole of the large house he came to the conclusion that no one was coming back, it had been completely torn apart, nothing of any value was left. The families rooms had been savagely taken apart, the elegant clothes they had brought with them ripped to shreds, was it out of anger or malice he didn't know? There was no evidence of the slaughter in the main part of the house it was all confined to the cellar as if an execution had taken place ...that's when it hit him, he had been purposely sent away whilst the family were brutally murdered, it had been rumoured amongst his fellow comrades that he was in love with one of the girls he was guarding, they thought they had managed to hide it from everyone even her own tragic family. Obviously not hence his last minute trip to the city.

Running out into the grounds in a panic he ran around like a mad man trying in vain to find someone, anyone alive. It was only when he tripped over a mound of dirt did he realise the hell that he had stumbled on, literally. As he pushed at the dirt to get back up, he found his hand was touching another, only this one was cold, very cold and dead. For the next hour or so he frantically dug with his bare hands, out of respect as he didn't want to hurt the bodies with the blade of a spade. He found six bodies, six, there was supposed to be seven. The wounds inflicted were diabolical, some of the girls were unrecognisable. Tears streaming down his face he kept digging, he needed to find her. It was dark by the time he decided it was time to stop, her body wasn't there he didn't know whether to be elated or worried in case they had taken her alive for later.

Momentarily sitting back to survey the mess before him, he wretched at the sight of the bodies he had laid out side by side, covering their faces not just in respect but because the damage of the gunfire was so horrific he thought no one should have to stumble upon that. He couldn't take the bodies with him, where would he go, who would he talk to? Either way he was involved and he would be the only witness and surely not live long enough to tell the truth so he had to leave the family he once respected and loved behind.

Eventually his tears stopped, his dirty face streamed with their tracks. It was time to leave in case anyone returned, not that they would he was sure. He staggered to his feet, bowed his head performed the sign of the cross then scurried away as fast as he could.

That day was etched on Alexander's heart and mind for the many years that followed, he heard rumours that the family had escaped or some had survived, he knew only one may have survived, he had seen the other bodies. He tried in vain for many years to find her but all his leads led to nothing or threats on his own life.

Years past, the pain eased a little, enough for him to eventually move to Italy where he met and married a young Italian girl named Maria, they had a son Antonio. But secretly when he had enough money and the cold war a distant memory he hired a detective to try and find out what he could about the family in the house. He was an ex Bolshevik soldier like Alexander, but disturbingly within weeks of starting his investigation he disappeared, was this by choice or was he forced to?

The fear of all those years ago resurfaced, the sadness and guilt hung heavy in Alexander's heart. Unbeknown to him his wife Maria knew of his connections with the detective, she understood his pain, so much so that on her deathbed she begged their young son Antonio to promise one thing........

"Find your father's first love, find out what happened to her, find him peace."

From that day forward he made it his mission to find the peace his father needed, even after his death Antonio carried on looking for the young girl who first owned his father's heart.

Little did he know that the old regime would never give up either, one thing was for sure that if the truth ever came out Russia would never be the same again.

A soldier's love for a young girl could bring Russia down even all these years after the embers of passion had cooled, and the want for war still lingered in the air.

Dust particles danced in the smoke filled air of the dimly lit office. The only sound was the deep rasping of the old man behind the oak desk, tubes in his nostrils aiding his breathing, forcing an old body to keep living long after it really wanted to stop. Vadim Yurovshy was of the old regime, not a man to go up against even now in his ill health.

Held in his boney fingers was a glossy catalogue, the colours so bright it stood out in such a drab dark room, it was filled with items for sale at the popular auction house Christie's. It was opened at the page of the main attraction, a beautiful faberge egg reportedly once owned by Anastasia Romanov. Her parents had it created especially for her 16th birthday. Little did they know she would only have a year to appreciate it until tragedy struck and Russian history was made, for all the wrong reasons.

Slowly he ran his tobacco stained fingers over the colourful glossy picture, greed, bitterness and hate surged through him once more as he spat out the words.

"Buy it."

"Do you think it will lead us to the truth comrade?" The man in the dark suit shuffled from one foot to the other nervously as he questioned the old man who in turn replaced the brochure onto the desk as he slowly turned his dark sunken eyes to him, the man in the suit instinctively drew in a sharp breath, fear and apprehension raced through his body and mind all at once.

Struggling to answer as the oxygen slowly seeped into his old body from the machine he gripped the desk for support.

"The myth tells us of 'The Golden Teddy Bear' which in turn should lead us to what happened to the girl" As bitter excitement filled his chest he struggled once more to breath, coughing to such an extent alerting a male nurse who came rushing in to his aid. He still managed to wave the young man out of the room with the words "Buy it, buy it."

A cold misty rain fell slowly onto Tim's windscreen, his wipers moving just as slowly to wipe away the moisture that gathered impairing Jack's vision and view of the auction house. Both man and taxi witnessed two men in long heavy black coats and fur hats, hands rammed into their pockets against the cold weather stomping towards the building. As they approached the doorman they stopped, words were exchanged then the two men turned on their heels and stomped away quicker this time and not looking happy.

"Russian's" Both man and machine blurted out simultaneously.

"Hardly hiding the fact that the Russians are interested are they Tim?"

Tim's engine purred quietly as he watched the two men walking away recording their faces on his inbuilt computer system, running them through the MI5 data for facial recognition……a red warning sign appeared but no information was attached which meant only one thing…..their identities were on 'a need to know only basis'……..these are dangerous men, why would they be at an auction house?

As Tim pondered this question Jack sat up alerted to an old man's arrival.

Jack's gaze followed him as he made his way along King Street, he seemed sad, his hands in his pockets as if in resignation of an emotional defeat. He also came across as edgy, nervous as he constantly looked around as if he felt he was being followed. Jack looked around but there were only a few people milling about, no one out of the ordinary apart from the two Russians…….the Russians! The two men had stopped at the end of the road and were also watching the old man only they weren't hiding the fact.

When the old man reached the entrance to the auction house he turned for one last look around, Jack could see even from this distance the colour drain from the man's face as he and the Russians made eye contact. The taller of the two put his arm out to stop the very short one as he motioned to approach the old man who in turn noticeably flinched, stumbling a few steps backwards in fear he managed, just, to regain his composure and balance as he then almost ran inside the building.

Jack continued to watch as the old man vanished whilst the two men in black walked in his direction.

"The facial recognition identifies the old man as Antonio Strekotin the owner of Alexander's Toy store on Oxford Street, definitely a person of interest......to MI5"

"If the two Russians following him are as interested as I think they are then the old man Mr Strekotin is not as innocent as you think, MI5 have had him under surveillance for some time. They're not sure why but because the Russians are so interested they've set up a major surveillance on him to find out what he knows or has what the Russians want"

"Mr Strekotin's store is named after his father, an ex Russian soldier who escaped the 'old regime' when he was about 18 years old apparently he was an interest to the Russians then and his son Antonio has in turn moved around all his life. But the Russians have always been a few steps behind."

"Antonio must be getting on a bit, how can anyone live that long with the Russians on their tail?"

"The clues are there Jack"

"What clues?"

"Sometimes I wonder who the detective is here! The old man's father was a Russian soldier, he was 18. Think of the dates. Russian men have been following him all his life and his father and now where are we and why?"

Jack digested the 'clues' glancing at the huge advertising banner outside of the auction house. His eyes widened with realisation as the penny or should I say the egg dropped.

"The Russian royal family."

"Exactly, Antonio's father was a Bolshevik soldier at the time of the revolution and…massacre of the royal family."

"But they all perished. What would his father have or know that's so important to the Russians?" Jack fidgeted in his seat, curiosity and excitement overwhelming him.

"If we knew that Jack……." Tim stopped abruptly as two very elegant women slowly exited a fellow black London taxi that had pulled up outside Christie's.

The older of the two averted her gaze from paying the cab driver to look up at the giant image of the russian faberge egg.

Jack gasped as he looked from the woman to the egg and back again.

"What the hell?"

"It's time Jack." Tim's voice was soft as if an old friend had arrived, perhaps they had!

"Time for what?" Jack didn't take his eyes off the women.

"Time for the secrets to be revealed and an old score to be settled."

Tim quietly said to himself "And maybe bring Russia down"

"Huh"

"Jack you are about to see the history books rewritten." He started his engine.

The two women slowly entered the auction house, the older woman stopped and looked back towards Tim, Jack drew in a shocked breath as his eyes met the woman's. There was something about her he couldn't quite understand but a slight smile brightened her face as she bowed her head then followed the younger woman inside.

Tim smiled to himself, old friends, old scores a new history to be made.

Ever since Jack was a kid reading comics he had dreamt of being a detective, he became an officer in The Life Guards for ten years, following that he was a member of the SAS. His family were wealthy but he wanted to serve his country and work for his money. Aunt V gave him that opportunity when she recruited him for MI5 undercover work, he proved his worth very quickly as a top agent.

Aunt V as she was known worked for MI5 in a high profile position, very high. She was in charge of the department that trained Britain's top agents.

One particular night whilst Aunt V was having a quiet evening in the mews there was a loud knock at the door. Due to her training she made her way down stairs carefully, armed with a Walther PPK. opening the door slowly all she could hear was the sound of a midnight owl.....and the dull hum of an engine.

As she carefully crept outside into the bitter cold moonlit night air she saw no one except an empty London black taxi, it's engine running. Making sure no one was hiding close by she needed to decide what to do with it. Someone had left him for a reason, but why and who? Leaning against the warm engine she tried to make sense of the 'gift'. She reached inside to turn the engine off.

"My name's Tim by the way." Aunt V almost knocked herself out as her head shot up and hit the door frame at the sound of the body less voice. Looking around the empty street she drew her gun, her back to the taxi moving slowly never losing connection with the bodywork for some kind of protection. The few lights that glowed in the street were enhanced by the cold white moonlight, casting shadows of all sizes over the cobbles. Aunt V's breath exhaled white in the night air heavy with anticipation of danger. Just as she slid along the body work back towards the warm bonnet she heard the voice again.

"I wouldn't worry there's no one about, only you and me Miss V, would you mind not leaning on my paintwork I'd hate for you to scratch it."

Aunt V shot round gun aimed at........the taxi!

"As I said my name is Tim, I thought you could do with my help."

That was over thirty years ago. Tim and Aunt Verene formed a solid bond, getting around London quickly and legally on many MI5 missions.

When she disappeared under suspicious circumstances her home and loyal friend Tim were automatically handed over to her nephew Jack Courage, who had done her proud with his loyalty and ability as a fellow member of MI5.

With Aunt V gone it was the first time he knew of Tim, she had managed to keep him a secret from everyone, even her colleagues, for years. He moved in one sunny morning, whilst tidying up he decided to take some box's down into the garage, the door was a bit stiff, arms full he pushed with his back almost falling into the dark dusty room. Steadying himself he picked up the bits and pieces that had fallen onto the floor. Looking up as he crouched he noticed a vehicle covered in a dirty sheet, thinking nothing of it only that it must have been his aunt's car he carried on gathering what he had dropped.

"Steady Jack, watch my paintwork!" Tim joked.

Jack stopped, his hand hovering mid air, guarded he looked around for the person who belonged to the voice. He realised he was alone or so he thought, slowly drawing his gun he crept around Tim unaware that it was he who was talking.

"There's no one else here but you and me Jack, you can put the gun away."

Jack stood stock still, gun in hand, eye's wide and looked in the direction where the voice was coming from, ripping the sheet off of the taxi he smiled to himself, Tim's lights brightened and dimmed, his way of a hello.

Only Aunt V could have a taxi in her garage, but how the hell could it talk?!

That talent was only the beginning and the start of an amazing partnership, another great bond was formed.

MI5 really did have a lot to answer for.....or did they?

# CHAPTER ONE

Jack stood admiring the beauty of the Faberge egg that sat before him, his roll as a taxi driver was a cover for his real occupation, no not working as security in an auction house, he was a private investigator who also worked for MI5.

The gold and royal blue egg which was protected by a glass case glistened in the light of the main auction room. It was the last egg owned by Anastasia Romanov, given to her on her sixteenth birthday by her parents. Inside was the most beautiful tiny golden teddy bear.

The value of the egg was way over 8 million but could go for a lot more depending who was to bid this afternoon, there were bidders from all over the world, in house and via the phones and internet, so this could turn out to be a long process.

Jack had men stationed all around the building inside and out, this was not just any Russian egg, it had been smuggled out of the house where the family were imprisoned before their execution, no one ever knew by who but their deaths made the value shoot up. With the rumours of survival and the subsequent appearance of the egg there was talk that the Russians were beginning to panic, why, no one had any idea but the one thing that was certain 'The Truth' could bring the Russian regime old and new crashing down with a lot of casualties.

The Russians of the old regime would do anything to get their hands on the egg, even kill for it.......or so Jack was led to believe.

In the darkness of the doorway of the packed room stood another mystery man, dressed head to toe in black.

His eyes twitched behind the blackness of the sunglasses with anticipation as they caught sight of the gold lights silently ricocheting off the stunning casing of the egg.

Nearby on another plinth in the shadow of the egg sat almost unnoticed a tatty teddy bear which once had been as golden as the Russian egg and was worth even more, if only the Russians knew and why.

Two teddy bears, one real gold and hidden inside a valuable egg the other threadbare and not so gold anymore and rather sad looking.

Tim sat outside watching who entered the auction house, no one was sure who was after the egg, how, when or if they would steal it but knowing the Russians were so interested Jack and Tim narrowed it down to them having a hand in the anticipated drama.

They were not to be disappointed today, King street where the auction house was situated seemed to be overrun by Russians, men dressed all in black standing out like sore thumbs, not even hiding the fact they were interested!!

The auction was to start at 10.30, at 10am the Russians took their positions at the back of the auction room. Jack and his men were on alert, they all exchanged knowing looks as the auction began.

It took less than twenty minutes for the sale of the egg, 15 million pounds, purchased by the short fat man in black seen earlier, accompanied by the tall, thin man in the same regalia. No one knew who they represented but assumed due to their accents and obvious black clothing they had connections with the Russians, or was it just another Russian billionaire wanting a faberge egg for their own private collection?

The next lot was the tatty teddy bear also of Russian origin but no one knew who had owned it just that it was rumoured to have been found discarded in the grounds of a garden of where the royal family had supposedly holidayed so it was valuable by association only......as far as Jack knew, an interesting coincidence?

Sat at the back of the auction house was the unassuming old man, rather sad looking and apprehensive. For some reason he caught Jack's eye again, he didn't look like he had the sort of money that would buy anything here today, but looks can be deceiving and he did after all own Alexander's toy store on Oxford street.

He hadn't shown much interest in the egg, although his face seemed to sadden a little more when it was brought out on show for the bidding. It was only when the tatty teddy bear was brought forward did he show any sign of real emotion. Sitting up in his seat more animated than before. Bidding paddle in one hand the other gripping the seat back in front of him so much so his knuckles turned white.

The bear was so worn and threadbare, dull of all colour, the only shining light in this lot was the golden belly button. The old man started bidding for it, Jack watched as the two women he had seen earlier getting out of the taxi who were now in the front and had also begun to bid. The look of desperation on the old man's face for some reason pulled at Jack's heartstrings, he looked from the old man to the women and back. Who were these people and why did they want the bear, no one else seemed to be bidding.

SOLD! For three million pounds, how did he have so much to spend and why would such a tatty bear be worth so much?! Was it just expensive sentimental value?

The old man seemed elated, the older of the women was equally crestfallen. Jack watched as she rose from her seat and gracefully walked towards the old man and spoke to him, surprise, confusion and fear crossed his face as she leant down to talk to him. A look of shock crossed the old woman's face as she seemed to notice something which Jack couldn't quite make out due to the distance between them, but the look was gone as quick as it appeared. As she spoke to him every Russian edged a fraction forward, was this the moment when they were going to make their move?

Jack could see the shock on the old man's face as the two women walked away, he looked like he had seen a ghost, his paddle fell to the floor, not once did he take his other hand off the chair in front, he needed the support.

Jack radioed through to Tim from his wrist mike and filled him in on the events unfolding inside the auction house, never once taking his eyes off the two women as they left or the old man. The women glided out of the auction room with grace and a mysterious air about them. The old man sat so still Jack began to think he had died until he nodded his head as if in conversation with himself.

At the same time Tim was witnessing a mass exodus of Russians leaving the vicinity. He wasn't sure who to follow until he saw the short fat man exit with the tall thin man, one of them was carrying a large Christies box presumably the egg was inside.

Tim was quick to act and drove up to the two men and spoke to them.

"Taxi gentlemen?" The dividing window inside Tim was black privacy glass so that no one could see there was no one actually driving. The men would assume that the voice was coming from the 'driver'.

The two Russians got in and asked to be taken to The Russian Embassy in Kensington.

So the egg was not bought by a Russian billionaire but possibly the Russian government. Why would the very government who murdered the Royal Family want to buy the Tsarina's and Tsar's final gift to their daughter?

As Tim pulled up outside the embassy he was astonished it was still in use, still standing actually as it looked uninhabitable, a demolition ball looked like it would improve the place tenfold. The windows looked like they could do with a good clean and plaster was falling off the exterior walls. Men in dark clothing paced the inner grounds quietly even at night, not a sound could be heard just the hum of distant traffic, no birds flew above, silence engulfed the taxi and the surrounding area.

In a downstairs window he could just make out an old man sitting gazing out, as he saw the two men get out of Tim his grim face lit up, then someone came up behind him and moved him away from the window, he was in a wheelchair.

Tim moved slowly away from the curb in case he could see anything more. As he drove away he caught a glimpse of something or rather someone who could be of use to him and Jack lurking in the grounds as if he was watching and taking in every movement, every coming and going.

# CHAPTER TWO

Antonio sat down at the back of the room, he didn't want to bring unwanted attention to himself. He had noticed the place was overrun by Russians presumably after the egg, he felt uneasy at the thought but there were very few people in this world who would know the truth about the bear so he felt safe to buy it. Or so he thought, he glanced over towards the front of the room and his heart almost jumped into his throat.

There were two women at the front who looked familiar, even from behind they emulated elegance of a different era, it must be a coincidence so he put it to the back of his mind for now, until the bear was brought forward. His heart stopped momentarily, at last his father may be on his journey of peace. What?!!! Why are the two women bidding? The coincidence was now looking weak, very weak.

He was bidding against the two women, no one else was interested in the bear. Panic rose in him as he kept raising his paddle. The relief on realising his final bid of three million had been accepted was overwhelming. He slumped in his chair, soon noticing a shadow cast over him as someone stood in front of him he looked up. Oh my lord he thought the likeness was too much to be a coincidence now, in fear he began fiddling with the small signet ring on his little finger. The old woman's face crossed with shock as she noticed the ring. Leaning in closer to him she spoke quietly, almost too quietly for his old ear's....

"Look after the bear Sir, there are many others than myself that want him. You and I want him for the right reason, they don't. They are dangerous and will stop at nothing to get him back, nothing, stay alert, stay safe....please....oh my!!"

She gasped as her eye's caught sight of the signet ring more closely. Her haunting eyes looked into his, a single tear rolled down her old but beautifully elegant face, then she was gone.

Once he composed himself he turned around, the two women were nowhere to be seen but the remaining Russians were staring at him, fear overwhelmed him, he felt as if the room was closing in on him, almost fainting he steadied himself with the back of the chair in front of him.

"Sir would you like to come with me and we can deal with the payment for the bear. Sir Sir are you ok?" The young man put his hand on Antonio's shoulder, he looked up at him. "Yes of course, of course, thank you." Antonio silently creaked as he got up out of his seat and made his way to the office, he felt the eyes of the Russian's burning into his back as he walked away, even without looking he could sense them inch forward hesitantly as if to follow him.

Jack again called through to Tim, not once did he take his eyes off the old man and the Russians, Something bothered him......but what?

"Tim, can you run another check on Antonio Strekotin for me please, he's just bought The Golden Teddy Bear for three million pounds?"

"Sure Jack but I thought we were here for the egg? By the way I've just taken it and it's buyers to their destination, the buyer isn't a Russian billionaire......it's the Russian government."

"What? Well that makes it all the more interesting." Jack was slowly seeing pieces to the puzzle forming but the 'picture' wasn't clear yet.

"The only bidders for the bear was Mr Strekotin and the two women we saw earlier entering the building, sadly I have no way of finding any info on them as they didn't buy anything, but they seemed to know Mr Strekotin in some way although he was surprised to see them, almost frightened. We'll have to get that information from him as soon as we can."

"I'll get onto Strekotin ASAP Jack, meet me at home I've got a little job to do before I get back." With that Tim was off into the lunch time traffic to hunt for an old friend.

# CHAPTER THREE

Antonio hailed a taxi as he exited the auction house, slumping back into the cold leather seat he let out a tired old breath of tense relief. He hadn't noticed the two Russians peeling off from the group of fellow comrades that had been waiting outside.The two followed closely behind until he reached his destination, his store, Alexander's on Oxford Street.

Still clutching the packaged bear as if his life depended on it which at this precise moment it probably did he scurried down the rubbish strewn alley at the side of the department store towards the staff entrance. He stopped to fumble in his pocket for the keys, as he pulled them out he dropped them. Crouching slowly due to his old age he turned his head to the left, sensing he was being watched. He gasped as he saw two men in black just stood there not even hiding the fact they were watching him. Without looking as his hands scurried around until they located the dropped keys, he got up as quick as his old body would allow and managed to get the key into the lock and open the door. Shutting it behind him he lent his sweating head on the cold steel of the door, fear gripped his old heart. Russians at the auction house, then the two women and now more Russians here at his store.

This was no coincidence...........it had begun.

He needed to act quickly, his late father had warned him of his own countrymen, especially where the bear was concerned. He needed proper protection and he knew just who to call, he carried in his wallet a tatty business card his father had found one day in a taxi, he had been told to use it when needed but would never say who told him, another question to be answered one day, perhaps soon.

A hand grabbed his shoulder, his old heart almost gave out, he turned clutching the package closely to his chest which thankfully still held a beating life organ albeit a bit faster than it should have been.

"Father are you alright? You look like you've seen a ghost."

"I, I think I have Alex I think I have. I need to make a phone call, I'll be in my office and I don't want to be disturbed." Antonio scurried off leaving his son open-mouthed watching him enter his office then listening to him locking the door behind him, something he had never seen his father do, ever, something was wrong.

"Hello is that Mr Courage of Courage Security?" he practically whispered down the phone, he slumped in his chair on realising he had got to Jack's answer service, he didn't leave a message, there must be no trail for the Russians to follow.

# CHAPTER FOUR

Tim drove around the city towards the Harrods department store, he had a feeling the one person he was looking for would be round the back, and sure enough there he was.

Robbie The Rat was minding his own business, rummaging around in one of the large bins at the back of the store. All Tim could see was his ample bottom sticking out feet in the air and the sound of chomping. Since his last escapade with Tim and Jack he'd got the taste of the good life, and where else could you eat like a king for free?

"Robbie, Robbie" Tim shouted down the dimly lit alley.

Struggling to lift himself out Robbie looked back up, caviar and blue cheese smeared round his mouth. He grinned as he saw 'his brother in arms' his fellow soldier who almost caught a diamond thief, what an adventure that was, they may not of got their man but it was one hell of a ride.

"Tim hey it's great to see you. You got another job for me?" He wiped the expensive Russian caviar from his mouth, ironic I know!!

"Yes Robbie, I can get you Russian caviar fresher than that!"

"Oh wow, great what's the job mate?"

"I need you to get into the Russian embassy and find some info out for me, Boris will be waiting for you to show you around inside."

Robbie jumped in, Tim drove off with a very excited rat in the back, that was until they pulled up outside the embassy.

Robbie stopped talking his mouth fell open at the sight of the decaying building in front of him.

"Yikes, are you sure people actually live in there it looks like it should have been condemned years ago?"

Tim dropped Robbie off and watched him scurry towards the side of the embassy, then he drove away and into the busy city traffic with the intention of going home.

# CHAPTER FIVE

Antonio put the bear in the shop safe, he stopped a moment and rested his hand on a tatty file that lay on the bottom, it was a thin file, as he slipped it into a secret compartment the feeling of regret washed over him, so many years had past there was so little info in there, but what was, was going to be big on impact if not in size.

He locked the safe then unlocking the office door he ventured out into the store, he could hear his son Alexander pottering about somewhere in the distance. Antonio was old fashioned, he liked to shut on a Thursday. As he stood surveying his achievement he noticed two large dark shadows creep over him, the shelves and the floor, stopping at the large front window covered in a red blind embezzled with a giant 'A' for Alexander's. Panic gripped him, he hadn't realised how far into the shop he had walked, the office seemed to be further away than he thought. The door moved as it closed with a click. There was only supposed to be himself and Alex here today, slowly he crept back towards the office anticipating someone jumping out on him.

His old hand touched the metal of the door, cold to the touch as he pushed it open to reveal...........

"NOOOOOOOOOOO!!!" Antonio slumped to the floor at the sight of the open safe, empty, the bear was gone!!

Alex came running as fast as he could to find his father in a heap on the floor almost sobbing the words "They've taken him, those damn Russians have taken him"

"Who father who, what Russians?"

Antonio's demeanour changed in a split second, a darkness filled his eyes, his voice calm and meaningful he grabbed his son's shoulders as he stood slowly.

"I need you to call Jack Courage, I should have left a message, call him now and get him to come here." he shoved the tatty business card into Alex's hand.

"Why father why?" Alex was confused at his father's distress.

"Because he's the best detective in the country and I need him to find my bear, her bear."

With that he slammed the office door shut in Alex's face and locked it again while he waited for Jack.

# CHAPTER SIX

Jack met Tim back at the garage below his mews.

"Antonio Strekotin is the owner of Alexander's the old fashioned department store on Oxford Street as we already know" With that Antonio's face appeared on the large plasma screen on the wall, all the information that Tim had was there in front of them to read, sent from his on board system straight through to the computer table then onto the large screen in front of him and Jack to study together. It was like a giant IPad connected to all government systems with or without their permission or knowledge.

"He's of Russian descent, that's interesting Tim."

"Not half as interesting as who his father was." Jack scanned the screen to see what Tim had seen

"Alexander Strekotin, same name as his grandson, well that's traditional but not unusual."

"Jack look closer, look at his last commission as a soldier." Jack moved closer to the screen, his eyes grew bigger in surprise.

"A bolshevik soldier, not just any Russian soldier whose last commission was guarding a wealthy family at a country house. He was eighteen at the time." Jack turned towards Tim, his mind working overtime.

"A Bolshevik soldier, a wealthy family and a bear?" Jack was putting some details together out loud.

"A large house, the bear was found in the grounds where it was also alleged that a whole family had been executed there but no actual details as yet. It looks like they have been purposely deleted from the system to hide the identities of the victims, but why?"

RING RING the phone snapped Jack out of his thoughts.

"Jack Courage of Courage Security, how can I help?"

"My name's Alexander Strekotin, I need your help" Jack almost dropped the phone, Tim's headlights flicked onto full beam in surprise as the phone conversation connected to the sound system on the plasma screen so that he could hear everything.

"How can I help?" Jack looked at Tim who in turn flashed his lights questionably.

"My father has been robbed, someone broke into his office and stole............." He stopped talking.

"He stole what sir?" Jack waited, silence suddenly broken by a confused voice.

"A teddy bear, they stole a teddy bear sir. I know it doesn't sound important but my father has just purchased it for.........

"Three million pounds" Jack and Alexander simultaneously announced the value!!

Jack raised his eyebrows at him, Tim who in turn quietly said.....

"Coincidence?!" His headlights dimmed and brightened as he thought things through, scanning the details on the screen in front of him. Things were moving quicker than he had expected, the Russians were obviously onto something and not wasting any time by stealing the one thing that no one realised was actually important, they had the egg and now they had the bear but still no one could actually make a valid connection between the two items.

"I'd better get back to the embassy and check in with Robbie. The Russians are more involved than we first thought, if he's in danger then he needs to be forewarned." Tim waited until the doors rose and then drove as fast and as legally as he could, he needed to get to Robbie before the Russian's realised there was more of a connection between the egg and the bear, that's if they could, why would there be a connection? If he and Jack hadn't made it yet he was sure as hell the Russian's hadn't.

# CHAPTER SEVEN

It was early evening now and the traffic was full of office workers hurrying home via buses and the underground, tourists hailing fellow London taxis for pre theatre drinks or because they were exhausted after hours of sightseeing and shopping.

The light was dimming and rain slowly began to fall again, then increased to a downpour. As Tim reached the embassy the eerie silence still hung in the air and a heavy darkness had fallen over the crumbling building, the dirty windows darker than ever with the only light coming from the same downstairs room as before which still looked dull and unwelcoming and frankly quite haunting.

Tim drove right up to the side entrance and tooted his horn. It was a few minutes until Robbie came running out from behind the bins.

"Hi Tim, no sign of anyone yet mate, I wish they would hurry up. I'm getting cold and could do with a bite to eat." He hugged himself against the weather which had turned nasty now, Tim opened his side door to let his little friend in, meanwhile he radioed through to Boris.

"Boris where the hell are you? Robbie's been waiting hours for you to let him in."

The radio crackled, it sounded like a bad line. Eventually a deep voice with a Russian accent came through.

"I am sorry Tim but the place is suddenly overrun with men, it's as if the Russian army as invaded my ome country again. I am coming now comrade tell your friend to meet me at the back of the bin area, I will be there momentarily."

Boris clicked off line, Robbie got himself together and jumped out into the cold rain again. Waving to Tim he ran off back towards the bins, oh the high life.

It was the cleanest one he'd ever seen, while he was waiting for his contact he had a look around and inside the bins. WOW he thought every bit of paper had been shredded and shredded again, there was no way anyone would decipher anything in there! The whole area smelt like it had been scrubbed to within an inch of its existence with bleach, nothing incriminating was going to be found here no matter how hard you looked.

The night was getting darker, there were no outside lights, the mixture of darkness and silence was creeping Robbie out as he sat behind one of the bins making him more and more impatient. Cold rain water gushed out of a broken drainpipe adding to his increasing discomfort.

"Hello, you must be Robbie." Robbie shot round at the deep voice, but he couldn't see anyone, he scanned the area, it was taking a while for his eyes to grow accustomed to the darkness. It seemed to be coming from the shadows, two big eyes followed the voice out of the darkness, behind them was the round face of a large rat with an even bigger grin.

"My name is Boris, I am Russian rat, I am at your service." He held out his hand to shake Robbies. He was taller than Robbie and very round, boy did he have a grip on him!!

"Yep I'm Robbie, pleased to meet you Boris. Got any caviar, I'm starving?"

"Hahahaha that's my boy, come on let's get you inside before someone sees you hahaha caviar" Boris put his arm around Robbie and laughed all the way as they made it to the inside of the embassy basement.

Once there the atmosphere appeared even darker than outside if that was possible, the condition of the place wasn't as clean as the bin area which seemed odd to Robbie. The cold that hung in the air inside seemed to penetrate his wet fur, he shivered, it didn't help that he was still soaked from the rain. Boris looked at him and grinned fondly, slapping him on the back almost knocking him over, he didn't know his own strength!

"Come wiz me my comrade I av something that will warm you up hahaha"

Soon Robbie was coughing on a large vodka, but at least he was as promised warming up!!!

Once Robbie was comfortable Boris rounded up some of his men. They all slowly made their way through the dimly lit basement corridor towards the stone steps leading up to the ground floor where the main hallway was situated.

Boris was first to sneak a look around the doorway, the vast black and white square tiled floor looked even bigger to him being a rat.

He motioned for the other's including Robbie to follow, first of all he put his finger to his lips... "Watch your claws on the tiles, they will make noise so please be very careful." He tiptoed into the tiles, tip tap tip tap, one by one his men followed. They reached the bottom of the stairs, seeing a light coming from one of the rooms at the front to the left of the main door Boris signalled for everyone to halt, Robbie being Robbie wasn't concentrating and crashed into the back of him, the two of them fell to the floor noisily instantly getting up shushing each other! The other men froze in fear, panicked at the anticipation of being discovered.

They stopped as an angry voice boomed out of the lit room, it looked like a mist wafted out, but when it reached the men they grimaced at the strong smell of Russian cigarettes, Robbie was about to cough, Boris shoved his hand over his new friends mouth making his cheeks balloon panic rising in his eyes. He sneakily blew the smoke out of the side of his mouth and grinned sheepishly as Boris removed his hand....then coughed quietly!

Tiptoeing nearer to the open door where the angry voice was coming from they craned their necks to look around the wooden door frame. Inside was a large beautifully carved desk, sat behind was an old man in a wheelchair, plastic tubes in his nostrils to aid his breathing which Robbie thought odd as he was puffing away on one of the strong disgusting smelling Russian cigarettes. In front of him stood two men, one tall and one short and fat who both seemed to be physically shaking, and not from the cold outside!

The air was misty due to the smoke and old particles of dust floating around, the place looked like it hadn't been cleaned in decades. The only lighting came from an old fashioned lamp that looked like it was running on gas, Robbie thought it probably was.

He strained to hear what was being said, something about two women at the auction, and two teddy bears.

The old man's voice rose so it was more audible to Robbie and everyone else.

"What do you mean two teddy bears?" The old man's eyes suddenly livened up at the mention of two bears.

The taller of the two men placed the tatty bear on the desk in front of the old man who coughed loudly which soon turned into a choke, Robbie and Boris held their breath waiting for the old man to keel over!! He managed to regain some composure.

"Why av you brought me this.....toy?" The anger and disgust in his voice sent shivers down the men's spines.

"Well commander Yurovshy the bear was rumoured to have been found in the grounds of the House, we thought it might have some significance, especially as an old Russian and the two Russian women were in a bidding war for it."

The two men looked at each other with their mouths open, scared as the old man seemed to ponder the information as his eyes bored into them.

The tall thin man reached inside the box to retrieve the egg and placed it gently onto the table. The old man grabbed it, his weak fingers struggled with the clasp until it flipped open to reveal a tiny bear inside.

The fat man spoke. "What is so important about the egg if I may ask commander?"

The old man didn't answer straight away, eventually looking back up, his eyes deep set with old age and illness, dark with evil intention.

"This is the last gift that idiot gave to his not so innocent daughter, Russian legend has it that the bear is the clue to the whereabouts of the one that survived" He grabbed the tatty toy bear and threw it onto the floor.

Boris and Robbie looked at each other quizzically, 'what daughter, what survivor?'

"We won't be needing that, why the hell did you get it anyway?"

"It was the Lot after the egg, as I said it was sold to an old Russian man a Mr Strekotin for three million pounds, we didn't know if there was any importance of the bear but when this one came up we assumed it was too much of a coincidence and followed him to a store and well er we er stole it off of him. Have we made a mistake Sir?"

The old man stopped looking at the egg almost dropping it. Quietly he spoke...

"What did you say the old man's name was?" His deep penetrating eyes darkened, if that was possible.

"Er Strekotin Sir." The tall man's voice almost faltered in fear that stealing the scruffy toy was a mistake.

Cautiously the tall thin man bent down to pick the bear up off the floor. Boris had crept in and as the man grabbed it their eyes met as they both simultaneously reached for the bear Boris froze grinning in fear as his eyes bulged. The man in return was startled but soon forgot him as the old man shouted back at him. He was used to seeing rats running around the embassy! (however there are not many rats dressed in traditional Russian uniform!)

"What do you mean three million pounds, Strekotin.... Strekotin I know that name.....give me the bear now!!!" He grabbed the toy off of the man, his bony fingers grappling with it as he examined it roughly trying to find some sort of obvious value to it. Slamming it down onto his desk in frustration he shouted at the men.

"Strekotin is a name known to my father, he was at the house with a young soldier of that name, but not the day of execution.

But the boy did try and find out what happened to the family, he was very close to one of the girls, it was rumoured they were lovers and he gave her the bear. He was sent away so as to not get in the way when the family perished. Mmmm perhaps this toy does av some history to it. It's too much of a coincidence that Strekotin purchased the bear" Placing it on the desk to the side of him he stared at it for a few seconds.

"Leave me, I'm tired. No no leave the bear. If he paid that much for it there must be something more to it than we thought." He ignored the two men as they scurried out, Boris had regained the ability to move and was now stood with his back to the old desk trying to get Robbie's attention.

"Pst pst Robbie over ere now!" Robbie scurried in past the two men as they left throwing himself against the desk next to Boris. They looked at each other with surprise or was it fear or both?

"Now what?" Two pairs of eyes bulging with apprehension as Boris signalled with a nod of his head that the bear was above them, Robbie realised what he meant and looking back at him alarmed at the thought they were going to have to somehow get it off of the desk, the old man may be a problem but getting up there was the first hurdle...literally.

A couple of the other rats had joined them, Boris signalled for them to get on each other's shoulders like acrobats. Stretching like athletes and and quietly chanting 'huh huh' in unison one by one they jumped up and dragged each other on to their shoulders, although they did seem slightly out of practice, one of the rats slipped and dangled upside down momentarily, grinning as if it was part of 'the act'.

Boris gave Robbie a leg up, he scrambled up the men and as he reached the top of the last man he was within reach of the bear.

He leant forward and was just about to grab it as the old man's claw like hand made a grab for it without looking whilst he was reading a tatty old file, he got to the bear first leaving Robbie to fall flat on his face, almost immediately he felt someone grab his feet and whip him out of sight his fingers scraping along the desktop in panic, he fell backwards, dangling precariously upside down as the other rats held onto him, sweat pouring off their foreheads as they struggled to keep hold of his furry ankles, he slowly swung in mid air.

Just as they thought they had lost their chance to get the bear and with Robbie still dangling the old man started coughing again, this time it really took hold and he lost his grip on the toy as it fell to the floor whizzing past an upside down Robbie landing right in front of the tower of rats. Quick thinking Boris grabbed it and ran towards the door almost getting run over by a nurse as he ran in to help the old man as he started to turn blue!

Robbie had dropped to the floor as Boris being the base part of the tower of rats suddenly ran off! Luckily Robbie was caught by a waiting Russian rat and the others took this as their chance to get out without being noticed, running like the wind back into the hallway and ignoring the sound of tapping claws echoing in the air as they scurried almost skidding as fast as they could back towards the basement.

They all ran through the open door and ended up in a pile as they collided with Boris who had tripped over the bear and landed at the bottom of the steps winded.

Robbie grabbed the bear as the men grabbed Boris dragging him to his feet without even stopping, they all made a run for the back of the building skidding noisily on the old wooden floor boards too panicked to worry about the noise at this precise moment.

Crashing through the back door into the courtyard where the bins were kept, Robbie managed to keep the bear off the wet ground, it was bigger than him so it was a struggle. Boris and his men came crashing through the door stopping abruptly as they came face to face with the bear, sighing simultaneously as they noticed Robbie behind him. No one uttered a word, Boris shook Robbie's hand so vigorously as he still held onto the stuffed animal it shook with him.

"Until we meet again comrade, soon I ope" Robbie not wanting to stay longer than necessary smiled and ran for the exit.

Smiling they all waved him off as he ran towards the main road then stopped, there was no sign of Tim, Robbie began to panic, he couldn't be found outside with the bear. Just as he was thinking he was going to have to run up the road dragging it Tim pulled up at the kerb.

"Get in quick, well done Robbie you're a star" Robbie struggled to drag the bear in behind him falling backwards onto the floor then almost falling back out as Tim roared off up the road before Robbie hanging off the door frame had managed to get properly in let alone shut the door.

Tim was driving at a quite a speed in and out of traffic while Robbie was still hanging onto the taxi, the bear rolling about in the back eventually he heaved himself inside flat on the floor only to find the bear thud on top of him blocking out any light but this time he grabbed onto it and didn't let go. It wasn't long until they made it home to the garage and a waiting Jack.

Jack's face was a picture when he saw the bear struggling to get out, relieved as he noticed Robbie holding onto it from behind.

Laughing he gave Robbie a hand with the bear while Tim drove inside.

Jack placed the bear on the computer screen table, scanning it with a 3d camera sending the image to the huge plasma screen on the wall with a precise detail of the solid structure.

"Well there's nothing really unusual about it, the only unblemished bit is the golden belly button which has some Russian writing on it but I still can't quite make out what it says. It just looks like a piece of squashed metal"

Tim now parked in front of the screen took a good look at the picture, a voice behind him spoke up.

"The old man was annoyed that the men had stolen a tatty bear. Apparently it was found in the grounds of some house where a family were kept, the other bear which is inside some egg was supposed to be a clue as to someone who survived but he was confused as to how it would be, and who would of or could have survived, it's just a small bear inside of an ornamental egg" Robbie sat down on the couch and snuggled into a blanket to get warm.

Jack slowly turned to look at Robbie shocked at the amount of information, confused as to why the Russians would want an old tatty bear, but curious at the fact that the Russians actually didn't know the importance of it and didn't want it in the first place. Turning back to the screen to think he carried on talking.

"So the bear is a key in all of this but which one, surely the one inside the Faberge egg would be more valuable."

"Why would a young soldier get into trouble for falling for a young girl who was held hostage in a large house, he bought her the bear? She must have been someone important to be locked away, especially as he tried to find out about her after the execution." Robbie spoke matter of factly. Jack spun round open mouthed Tim's lights shone more brightly.

"What the hell are you talking about Robbie?"

He looked up at Jack "The soldier who was on guard in the house.....he bought it for one of the girls that was held there, his name was the same as the guy on your screen, Strekotin, but his first name was er I think er oh that's it Alexander.

I got a quick look at a page of the file when it was on his desk, I gotta photographic memory you know!! The old man is fuming that the Strekotin guy bought the bear, he had a bad coughing fit and we managed to get the bear out of there." Robbie saw the look on Jack's face and stopped talking feeling he had said something wrong. Quietly he asked "Does any of that help?" His eyes wide in fear of being in trouble.

Jack was speechless, Robbie had found out more info in ten minutes than Jack had found out in the last few hours.

"Tim, we need to go and speak to Strekotin first thing in the morning, he's expecting us. He wasn't feeling well earlier so asked me to go round to see him tomorrow once his blood pressure had stabilized. Robbie you make yourself at home, I'll get you some supper, I think you deserve it well done mate." Jack grinned at his furry friend who hadn't heard a word, he was fast asleep snoring his head off.

"Oh great just what I need, a snorer haha" Tim settled down for the night as well while Jack made his way up stairs to his bed. The Bear was safely locked away with the file Jack had set up on the case. The file was slowly growing in size but there still wasn't enough information.

# CHAPTER EIGHT

Outside in the dark, elongated shadows cast by the full moon along the cobbled road a man in black loitered, dragging on a cigarette that left a stench hanging thick in the air. His piercing eyes stared at the garage door knowing what lay behind, something so small and unassuming but it could still bring his mother Russia crashing down. All evidence of a possible survival had to be destroyed, blood had already been shed a little more won't matter.

Throwing his cigarette butt onto the wet floor the last of the embers hissing as they hit the rainwater he walked away into the night, into the beginning of another cold war.

# CHAPTER NINE

The next morning Jack and Tim made their way to ALEXANDER'S the toy store on Oxford Street.

Tim drove slowly down the rubbish filled alleyway stopping outside the staff entrance. Getting out Jack walked around the back of Tim, as he glanced up towards Oxford Street he noticed a man in sunglasses looking around the corner, Jack kept staring at him as he walked around Tim. The man stared back and moved blatantly into view, he was dressed head to foot in black.....Russian. A cold wind blew down the alley forming a mini tornado around the stranger.

Jack knocked on the door without taking his eyes off the man. He glanced away momentarily as Alex opened the door, when he looked back the man was gone.

"Mr Strekotin, I'm Jack Courage of Courage Security I'm here to see your father." He held his hand out to shake Alex's.

"Mr Courage thank you for coming, I'm sorry my father couldn't see you yesterday I think it was the shock of the robbery that brought on one of his attacks, thankfully he's better this morning. I'll show you to his office"

Alex and Jack walked towards the office. As he approached closer he noticed the door was open, an old man sat deflated at the desk, the same old man he witnessed purchasing an uninspiring bear for three million pounds. The same man now broken at the theft, if it was possible he actually looked older.

"Mr Strekotin." Jack spoke quietly, the old man slowly looked up at him, his eyes even sadder than Jack remembered.

As he looked behind Jack the very same eyes darkened at the sight of his son.

"Alex can you leave Mr Courage and I alone please?" Alex seemed confused even hurt at being left out of the meeting, he slowly closed the door not once taking his worried eyes off of his father, the door clicked closed and Antonio shot up out of his seat like a younger man, he went straight to the safe to retrieve the file from it's secret compartment.

"Mr Courage I need you to take this file and find the detective Sam Duggan, he is the only one who is in contact with the original owner of the bear. Well actually her descendents as she sadly could not be with us now. He will know however what happened to her and I need to find out that information, I am too old for this, but I made a promise to my mother on her deathbed to find her for my father"

"I'm confused sir, find who?" Jack sensed there was more to this nondescript bear than he realised but what? The old man approached him, determination and fear etched in his face all at once.

"The Russians must NOT keep the bear, they must never ever find out what happened to them or where her family are. Please find the bear, Sam Duggan will know what to do."

For some reason Jack kept it from the old man that he had the bear in his possession, for his own safety, the less he knew the better.

"Ok I'll call him, what's in the file sir." As Jack took it off the old man he noticed how thin it was, which didn't fill him with confidence. He thought his file was thin but this had even less in it!

"All you need to know is in there no more. Now please go and find Mr Duggan......before the Russians do." With that he turned his back and lent on the desk to steady his nerves, Jack took this to mean he was dismissed and left.

Closing the door behind him he came face to face with Mr Strekotin's son Alex.

"Excuse me Mr Courage can you please tell me what my father wanted?"

"I'm sorry Mr Strekotin I'm afraid I can't client confidentiality" With a feeling of guilt he left the son standing staring at him as he left the store jumping into Tim.

Tim sensed the worry in Jack, he kept quiet for a while as he turned around and made his way back onto Oxford Street filtering into the busy traffic.

"Home Jack?"

"Yes please, I've a few calls to make." He seemed to be in a thoughtful distant mood, he needed to find the detective Sam Duggan who knows more than what's in the file, which Jack found odd. Why was the file so thin, why didn't Mr Strekotin Snr have more information if Sam did?

"Why didn't you tell Mr Strekotin we have the bear Jack?"

"I thought he would be safer for the moment, the less he knows the better and we are one step ahead of the Russians." Jack gazed out of the window at the London architecture, wondering if they were being followed.

Back at the garage Jack scanned the paperwork and sent it to the screen so Tim could see it as well.

"Sam Duggan – Detective – witness of the murder of Paris multi millionaire Louis Bonaparte in a parisian park. Kidnapped and held hostage by Russians. Whereabouts now not known"

"Well that doesn't really help does it? The only connection is that he was kidnapped and held by the Russians it doesn't say why the millionaire was murdered. How in heaven's name are we going to find a man whose whereabouts are not known. Grrrr" Jack was getting frustrated, he threw the paperwork down onto the computer screen table as he did so a small photo fell out, smiling back sadly was a young girl.....a young girl holding a teddy bear. Jack hadn't noticed the picture fall out, Tim however did and a feeling of sadness and guilt washed over him, even he had the ability of emotions......well he is Tim The Taxi!!

# CHAPTER TEN

"Sam, I need you to contact a Mr Courage." The woman held the phone tightly to try and stop the nervous trembling.

"Why ma'am, is everything alright?" Sam sat staring nervously at the paper cuttings that covered the wall of his small bedsit, every time she called it made him wary, it always tempted fate and usually meant the Russians were close again.

"The bear has been located, it is back in the hands of my grandmother's first love's family but the Russians are not far behind, we need the bear Sam please. Mr Courage is the only man that can help us now."

Sam's stomach turned at the thought of the bear finally being found more so at the mention of the Russians. He agreed to contact this Mr Courage, he had to move quickly, if the Russians are already involved he has to move on yet again. He started packing his bag, he always travelled light ready at any moment to disappear into the lonely night again. He stopped momentarily to gaze at the beautiful woman in the faded photo, so much sadness for such a young girl to handle, so much fear to live with for so long. He had promised to put an end to such fear and put a heart to rest.

Grabbing his mobile phone he rang the number her Ladyship had given him. At the same time removing the cuttings from the wall, it was time to move on, his life depended on it, her life depended on it.

"Hello Jack Courage of Courage Security, how can I help?" Sam breathed a sigh of relief, he felt sure his nightmare was coming to an end, if only it was the end he had dreamed of.

"Hello my name is Sam Duggan, I've been asked to call you with information regarding a teddy bear. Can we meet to talk?" Sam waited as he heard a sharp intake of breath on the other end of the phone.

"Wow er yes Mr Duggan, I was just trying to find a way of contacting you. Where and when would you like to meet?" Jack couldn't believe what he was hearing, the coincidences were mounting by the second.

"Midnight in Covent Garden, I'll be carrying a large black holdall, I have a file for you, it's on a USB stick, I'll find you, we have to be careful, the Russians are close......." Sam stopped as he heard a noise on the stairs. "Too close........" Shoving paper clippings and his few belongings into the black holdall he carried on talking.

"Midnight Covent Garden please don't be late.....lives are at risk" Click the phone went dead, Jack was left with the receiver to his ear waiting for another sound, nothing.

Sam opened his window and throwing his bag onto the fire escape followed it as quickly as he could, the years of running had not been good to him plus the torture he had endured whilst the Russians held him hostage, he promised her he wouldn't tell, and he certainly paid the price. He made his way down the metal stairs as fast as his old battered body would allow, he knew they were here now, he knew he may not make it through the night but he had one last promise to keep to a beautiful lady with a beautiful heart. Running as fast as he could he heard the door of his room being kicked in and shouting, shouting in Russian.

Hugging the holdall close to his fast beating scared heart he ran into the rush hour of London commuters. His eyes darted all over the place looking for more Russians looking for someone to help him but no one could, not now, it was too late way too late.

He managed to find a dark alleyway where he could wait for Jack to meet him, constantly looking over his shoulder as he made his way from one dark hiding place to another, staying for no longer than five minutes in each, force of habit!

# CHAPTER ELEVEN

"Well this just gets weirder by the second. Tim we need to get to Covent Garden. Robbie get your mates to cover our backs please."

"Yes mate I'm on it." Robbie scurried off to round up the troop's.

"We are not waiting until midnight are we Jack?" Tim knew Jack so well, they were a great team, each knowing exactly what the other was thinking.

"No Tim we'll go now, it's a few hours early but I can guarantee he'll be close by, he's been on the run for so long he's not going to hang around for the Russians to get to him before we do. I'm intrigued as to what information he will have for us or will be willing to share." Jack dressed in all black, armed himself with his usual walther ppk, this one in particular belonged to Aunt V and never let either of them down. He hoped though he wouldn't have to use it tonight.

Dusk was falling quietly leaving a soft orange red glow in the sky. He admired the famous London skyline against the glorious colour, a skyline that hid so many secrets.

"Red sky at night shepherds delight. Let's hope this shepherd stays safe."

Slowly Tim drove away from the mews...... "Russian at three o'clock Jack"

"Yep I clocked him Tim, this is not going to be easy, try and lose him as best you can and then get to Covent Garden. We need to protect Sam, someone has to."

With that they drove off into the busy night traffic, Jack keeping an eye out for any Russians who may be hiding in the shadows of the capital city, a city that gives everyone a chance of a new life, but it can't protect them all.

# CHAPTER TWELVE

Tim and Jack slowly entered the cobbled area of the famous Covent Garden, people were still milling about, there were bars, pubs, theatres and of course The Royal Opera House nearby.

Jack had no idea what Sam looked like, only that he would have a black holdall with him, that really didn't narrow it down.

The sound of tyre rubber bumping slowly along the cobbles was all he could hear as Tim slowly manoeuvred around tourists and locals. He stopped near the back entrance of the opera house facing towards the Covent Garden Market, he was sure he saw someone lurking in amongst the pillars on the right hand side of the covered market, whoever it was looked nervous and was quite plump...no he was holding something close to himself, could it be a holdall Tim wasn't too sure.

"Jack I think I've found Sam, to the left halfway up amongst the pillars. It's him look he's coming towards us."

Jack jumped out of Tim and began to walk towards Sam, having to push his way through the few people left milling about. Jack lost sight of him momentarily when he saw him again there was a look of fear in his eyes, he held his hand up there was something in it. Jack sensed something was radically wrong and rushed up to him. As he reached him that's when Jack noticed the slight trickle of blood coming from Sam's mouth, he shoved something into Jack's hand then fell against him dropping the black holdall to the floor with a thud, he slipped down to the cold damp cobbles on top of the bag. That's when Jack saw the bullet hole in his back, kneeling with him he looked back to see two men in black coats. Realising they had been seen they turned on their heels and ran down New Row and out of sight.

"Tell them I'm sorry, please find them and protect them...... pleeease" Then the last breath left his body as he slumped lifeless into Jack's arms.

"Tim Tim please help me NOW!!!" Jack tried to hold Sam up without people realising he was dead "Come on mate I told you not to drink too much, haha" Luckily passersby thought he was just drunk, Jack managed to get him up and with his arm around him dragged him into the back of Tim, lying him on the floor out of view.

"Jack their back, they've brought reinforcements we've gotta get out of here now!" Tim shut Jack in with Sam and turned round driving off without bothering about the fact there was no driver. It was late and most people had had enough to drink not to notice. About twenty men in black ran towards them, momentarily blocked by a hoard of drunk revellers.

Jack sat with the poor man who held so much history in his mind, if only Jack knew the half of it, he'd be shocked........ but more importantly Russia would begin to fall with a domino effect and once that happened there would be no stopping the destruction of the Red country.

# CHAPTER THIRTEEN

Leaning against the back seat as Tim drove around Jack opened his hand to see what Sam had given him, wrapped around a USB stick was an old photograph. He flattened the picture on his thigh, it showed four beautiful young ladies and a young boy from some time ago, smiling. Jack sat up straight at what he saw, one of the girls was holding a small toy to her heart........it was a small teddy bear.....just like the one back home in his safe, almost! Unbeknown to him at the moment the young girl was similar to the small picture he had left on the floor by the computer table back in the garage.

"Where to first Jack, what do we do with Sam? Poor guy." Tim just drove around, there wasn't much traffic this late at night. They both decided it was best to drop in at the head office of MI5, Jack called ahead to Chief Gibson who almost jumped down the phone at him when the Russians were mentioned.

Driving down the secret ramp to the basement two men helped Jack quietly unload Sam's body and put him on a trolley, covering him with a white sheet out of some sort of respect. He followed one of the other men up to Chief Gibson's office where the Chief was waiting for him in his dimly lit room.

Silhouetted against the window, the capital city lights surrounding his shadow with the now deeper red glow Jack had admired earlier he turned slowly to face Jack as he walked in.

"I have looked into this Sam Duggan, the only information is regarding a kidnapping in Paris, a multi millionaire Monsieur Louis Bonaparte a long distant descendant of Napoleon who had the family wealth but not political opinions and he was married to.................. a young Russian."

Jack's face registered shock.

"I thought that would interest you. The Russians seem to have a lot to do with this case don't you think?" Gibson motioned for Jack to sit as he sat behind his desk. His elbows on the desk hands as if in prayer he touched his lips with his fingertips staring back at Jack. Jack was his best agent with his 'sidekick' Tim, a traditional London black Taxi, who had quite a few extra features.

Between the three of them and MI5 they had solved quite a few cases over the years, he knew Jack was the best for this one but had to warn him of the dangers of going up against a whole country, in this case Russia. The old regime was one you wouldn't want to cross in the past or present. There were still supporters out there that would stop at nothing and I mean nothing to protect their mother country. Sam Duggan's death tonight was proof of that.

"Why would the red's want an old tatty teddy bear Jack?" He leaned back in his seat, his hands still clasped in front of his face as he waited for Jack to speak.

Jack stared at the Chief trying to think, the only sound was the low hum of late night traffic and the ticking of a clock. Jack felt tension building as the ticking grew louder and louder. He cut the silence with relief as he spoke.

"To tell you the truth Sir I have no idea but they seem keen to get it back, if they're willing to kill for an old toy like that then it must have a hell of an importance."

"I don't think even the Russians know why they want it Jack, my sources tell me they thought the egg was more important but going after the toy bear seems to me they're clutching at straws.

Anything to do with the Ipatiev House is important to them obviously, even a toy found discarded in the grounds."

"Why the Ipatiev House Sir?" Jack stared at the Chief as he looked at him surprised he didn't know what he was talking about, although something niggled at the back of his mind that the name seemed vaguely familiar, something else niggled, Gibson seemed to know more than he was letting on.

"Your Russian Royal history a bit rusty then Jack?" He grinned at Jack as it slowly dawned on him what or rather who he was talking about.

"Oh my lord you don't mean Tsar Nicholas and his family do you, oh you do don't you?" That's why it was so familiar! There was only so much information in the paperwork he had and there was no mention of the house or which Royal family members, just that it had royal connections.

Jack sat back in his seat totally stunned, he knew the story of the executions of the royal family, everyone knew about the rumours of survival that were proved to be unfounded.

"Are you trying to tell me that someone actually survived that massacre? Surely not, history says that there was no way anyone could have survived the hail of bullets. And the rumour that Anastasia had was proved to be false."

He got up shocked and walked around the desk to look out of the window onto the sky line of the city, a city so large it could hide anyone, but it wasn't hiding just anyone now, was it hiding the true ancestors of the Russian Royal family, that would really be something to scare the Russians into going on a killing spree.

Who would guess a small unassuming tatty teddy bear could be such a big clue to the possible survival and now maybe the continuation of a Russian Royal bloodline.

But if someone did survive, which family member or member's and how, who helped them and is obviously continuing to do so?

Jack and Tim had the one clue that could change the history books forever and bring a whole country crashing down, but this wasn't any country. Russia was feared all over the world for many reasons known and unknown, he was going to have to watch his back from now on, he and Tim are now moving targets. Knowing the Russians they were good shots.......dam good shots.

Jack half turned towards a seated Chief holding out the photograph the USB stick was wrapped in, Gibson slowly took it and the look of shock crept over his face as he looked at the old crumpled picture then back at Jack, the one very important piece of evidence they could wish for and was needed was right here in their hands, if only they knew.

Gibson called an assistant to have it scanned and filed straight away so as not to lose it.

"Do you realise how important this is Jack? This confirms that the Tsars family or at least some of them may have survived."

"How does a photograph confirm that? I'm sure no one would have survived Sir, after all they have done the DNA tests of the remains that were found, even Anastasia was found there."

"Was she?" Chief Gibson spoke as if he knew different.

Jack walked back and dropped into his seat in shock, trying to digest the possibility that members of the most famous tragic Royal family might have survived after all. And may have actually kept the Royal bloodline going. No wonder the Russians want to know what is going on, but still how could a photograph or even an unassuming teddy bear solve the puzzle?

Plus why is Antonio Strekotin involved, obviously because of his father Alexander, but he was only a young soldier ordered to look after the Royal family and was sent away before the executions, but why was he sent away?

While Gibson waited for someone to come and collect the USB stick he inserted it into his system and copied the contents onto his personal computer in case anything was lost once it left his office and to eradicate any viruses, the picture he had been holding in his hand was the first thing to come up on the screen.

That's when Gibson and Jack noticed the teddy bear in the arms of one of the girls, it was easier to notice due to the size of the screen being bigger than the small tatty aged photo. Gibson's eyes widened as he looked at the bear then at Jack.

"It's the same as the bear I have in my safe at this very moment, but with one difference, the belly button Sir."

Gibson ran his fingers through his white hair in shock. "What do you mean?"

"In the picture there is no belly button just fur"

"Do you realise which one of the sisters is holding the bear Jack?"

"Er no Sir, I've only just got the picture as you know so I really haven't had time to study it."

"Jack the girl who's holding it is...................." He turned to the window, then slowly back to look at Jack.

"Sir?"

"It's Anastasia Jack, it's Anastasia."

The shocking realisation shot through Jack's body like a lightning bolt.

The myth was starting to become a reality.

Could Anastasia have survived after all?

No wonder the Russians wanted the teddy bear and are willing to kill for it.

Jack jumped up and was out of the door with the sound of Chief Gibson shouting after him wondering where the hell he was going.

He needed to get back home, to the safe and the bear. Jumping into Tim he tried to regain the ability to speak normally without leaving any details out so Tim was up to speed with what was going on.

"This case has just got deadlier Jack ." With that every piece of glass in the taxi suddenly had a second layer rise up from inside the mechanism of the doors, bullet proof glass to match the bullet proof metal bodywork. Tim needed to protect his friend and colleague more than ever now.

The Russians want the bear back, they have travelled around the world following it but always a few steps behind, now they were close, too close. Jack and Tim had no idea if the Russians knew of the importance of the bear but that wasn't important now. They have already killed without all the questions being answered, there's no telling who they will kill next.

Jack had luckily taken a copy himself of the USB stick whilst he and Tim were on their way to MI5, it was downloaded onto Tim's on board computer system. On the way home he listened to Sam's final message he had left on it for him last minute, he must have known he was close to being killed.

On the recording he sounded scared, really scared. In the background towards the end they heard muffled voices, poor Sam was recording till the very last second, the Russians were that close. Who was the woman on the recording he called ma'am? He was on the phone to her before he rang Jack, good thinking on his part to record the conversation, Tim could do a voice recognition on her and maybe find out her identity.

They arrived back at the garage in the early hours, silence lay heavy in the cold air. In the background you could hear a little traffic on The Bayswater road. Tim drove slowly towards the mews but his instinct and inhouse radar system told him they were being watched.

"Jack don't get out until we are inside please." The garage door rose slowly, Tim drove in but this time the door shot down at speed. There wasn't any time to lose and they needed all the protection they could get at the moment. At the same time as the garage doors shut, bullet proof shutters closed on all windows and doors. The mews was London's own little Fort Knox.

Jack jumped out and headed straight for the safe, relief washed over him as he opened it to be greeted by the bear. He took it out to hold it, slowly running his hand over the dull fur, his fingers rested on the golden belly button. So gold against such drab fur, but if it wasn't there in the picture where did it come from and why?

"Jack come on please, I've downloaded the USB onto the main computer."

Jack did as Tim asked and the screen was suddenly awash with pictures, scans of paperwork, list of identities the girls had taken on to hide themselves. One picture stood out amongst all of them it was unmistakable and the last known home of Anastasia (if in fact she was the one that survived) and her family.....Kensington Palace.

"Oh lord they were right here under our noses all along Tim."

"Back home with their rightful ancestors and descendants."

Queen Victoria was Anastasia's great grandmother on her mother's side. The contacts that Sam had for them was our very own Royal Family, Jack read on. MI5 had unknowingly been protecting the girls all these years. WOW Jack couldn't believe what he was reading, he picked up the phone to call Chief Gibson.

"Chief?!"

"I know Jack, I've just read some of the papers on the stick. Even we have secrets here, this is one that even I had no knowledge of............."

"Oh dear God Chief......."

"Oh my God Jack........" Simultaneously the two men read the one bit of information that would rock both of their worlds. There was one person in MI5 that knew of who had survived and helped protect her and her family...........Jack's Aunt Verene, she was the sole agent in charge of the girls!

"Jack are you ok?" Tim was calm, too calm. Jack turned slowly to look at him.

"You knew didn't you, you and Aunt V looked after them, you even had them in your cab didn't you?"

Silence.

"I'm sorry Jack I'm not at liberty to say. High security forbids me"

Jack lost his temper, which he never did especially with Tim.

"High security?! Which one survived, the least you can do is tell me that one piece of evidence?"

Tim was silent for what seemed like an eternity, he decided now was as good a time as any to break his years of silence if only to protect Jack, his colleague.........his friend.

"It was.......Anastasia Jack, Anastasia survived the massacre."

Jack lent against the computer table to steady himself, the shock of a historical survival and his 'best' friend letting him down was almost too much.

"Oh my God!" The distant voice of Gibson listening in on the end of the phone.

"How could you not say anything Tim, Sam may still be alive today if you had divulged this important bit of information, the fact that you carried the one woman the whole of the Russian government of the old regime was after and wanted to kill. The whole world wanted her survival to be true. How and why would you not tell me ANYTHING?!!" He shouted at his friend, he felt betrayed.

"I'm sorry Jack, but I did try and find Sam on my own. Surely you don't think I would leave him out there to die do you? He was always one step ahead of me as well as the Russians.

Sam was good at his job and evading myself and the enemy. Yes I did have a young Russian and her daughter as passengers, Aunt V could only trust myself and as you know I am well equipped to protect."

"What do you mean and her daughter?"

"I didn't just meet Anastasia, I had her daughter and granddaughter in the back."

"Oh lord.!" Gibson almost fainted at the latest info.

Jack bowed his head in frustration, there was still so much to learn from Tim even after twenty years with him. But this piece of information was way too much to cope with right now.

"Jack, Jack are you there, please Jack we don't have much time." The Chief shouted down the phone trying to get Jack's attention, he clicked the Chief onto loudspeaker. No matter how angry or let down he felt Tim was still his partner and the best, especially now he knew his connections with Anastasia.

"Did I just hear right Jack? Tim was working with Verene on this case?"

It took Jack a few seconds to reply.

"Yes Chief, Tim is now our only reliable connection to Anastasia and her descendents."

"She had a daughter Chief, and there's a granddaughter. Full disclosure from now on." Tim still sounded business like but there was a hint of regret in his voice as he spoke, regret for so many secrets, so many missed opportunities of solving the case had he brought Jack in sooner.

"Gee thanks." Jack spat out sarcastically, he bit his tongue as soon as the words left his mouth, he hated feeling like this towards his friend.

"Right I suggest you both report back to me now Jack, we've a lot to catch up on. The case is flagged up as Top Secret code RED which means in Verene's book only a few are allowed to know anything about the case. So at the moment it's just you me and Tim. Get back here ASAP Jack."

"Yes Sir" Jack disconnected from the system and grabbed the teddy bear plus the thin tatty file and got into Tim. Jack still didn't notice the small tatty black and white photo of Anastasia that had fallen to the floor. He drove back to MI5 headquarters in silence. Back in the underground garage, as they parked Jack set up the system so that Tim could hear everything discussed in the Chief's office so he would be able to join in on the conversations. The walls were incredibly thick in the building and sonic barriers were set up to stop anyone on the outside hacking in or able to use equipment that could hear and record but Tim had MI5 clearance and he could connect to all wavelengths.

"I'll see you when I'm finished Tim." His voice was quiet and calm, a little hurt.

Jack started to walk away but stopped with his back to his friend. Tim spoke softly.

"I'm so sorry Jack, I was going to tell you when the time was right but once Sam got in touch I knew it was out of my control and I needed to regain control but with his death I knew that was too little too late. Even I don't know if Anastasia's daughter and granddaughter are still at the palace. When Verene disappeared all the information and secrets were locked inside her computer system, even I couldn't get into her files and then the girls disappeared along with Sam.

Verene was the only person they trusted with their lives, once she was gone they trusted no one but Sam. They never knew about my capabilities."

Jack didn't turn round, he took in what Tim was telling him.

"I'll go and see the Chief." He walked away slowly.

Tim felt crestfallen he had hurt his friend, failed his friend.

Even Tim The London Taxi has feelings.

# CHAPTER FOURTEEN

Jack walked slowly up the stairs and back to Chief Gibson's office. Angry that if he had known Tim's involvement Sam may still be alive, another pointless death.

He sat with the Chief going through all the evidence on the USB stick, trailing through letters, passport photos for different identities that Anastasia used. There were a lot of references about the bear and how desperate she was to get it back. She mentioned many times 'if it wasn't for my golden bear I wouldn't be here'.

She wrote in what looked like pages of a diary how she adored Paris, the freedom and her husband Louis who she loved dearly but there was always a place in her heart for Sasha, who this was wasn't clear...yet, there was no record anywhere of a Sasha.

"There must be a diary somewhere with everything we need in it, that would be worth as much as the bear if not more." Jack spoke as if making a mental note to himself, and to Tim.

Her life changed the day the teddy bear went missing, along with a 'trusted' servant (Anna Demidova) who had travelled from Russia to look for her all those years ago. In one letter she wrote......

'I have never felt this betrayed since my own mother country tried to silence me with my family. The Bear is all I have of my love Sasha and what my sisters did for me. If the bear is ever found they will know I live, they will look for me and kill me all over again but this time my spirit will die with my body. Anna Demidova (the servant) knew of my escape, how I survived, my life is over I am sure, so tomorrow we leave for London my Louis and Alexandria (daughter)'

By the dates of the diary it was written the day before her husband was murdered while meeting Sam Duggan in a Paris park, Sam was also kidnapped that night. Ana and Alexandria left the next morning without her husband, without her friend, guide and protector.

But she always sensed that she was being followed.

# CHAPTER FITHTEEN

Jack and the Chief sifted through all the evidence into the early hours of the next day.

Tim sat in the underground garage feeling guilty, as the evidence was coming through to him he felt uneasy in a way as it was all old news to him. As Aunt V's silent partner (only silent when other people were around) he was privy to all information and events. In his position as a vehicle he drove Aunt V and the two girls, Ana and Alexandria about the streets of London, mainly in the darkness of the capital city. Aunt V would visit the girls at Kensington Palace on a regular basis to chat regarding the whereabouts of the bear and whether or not the Russians were close to finding them. There was never any actual information of Anastasia's survival or whereabouts, just the daughter and granddaughter, important details were missing, years of information left out, was that on purpose?

There were times when out and about on the night trips they felt they were being followed, men in big black cars with darkened windows tailing them in full view but never making that final move. Which in a way was even scarier, it's all very well knowing your enemies and keeping them close but this was ridiculous.

Even looking out of the windows of the Palace men in dark clothes could be seen in the park spying, they must have known they were inside but due to the heavy security they also knew they would never be able to get close to the girls.

"Sadly since your Aunt V disappeared no one has any evidence of the girls and their whereabouts, for all we know they may have moved on for their own safety.....Jack are you listening?"

Jack's face was pale as a realisation swept over it.

"I've seen them recently!"

The chief almost fell out of his seat as he shouted.... "WHAT?!"

"The auction, the two women at the auction, they spoke to Mr Strekotyn at the auction house when he bought the bear.... oh my lord they were there bidding for the very same bear.......... Anastasia's bear......"

"Anastasia must have passed away years ago if you go by all the dates, so they must be Anastasia's daughter and granddaughter. You know what this means?......The Royal bloodline is definitely still alive, alive and well in London. No wonder the Russians are now coming out of the woodwork. This is huge Jack, huge!"

Jack slumped back into his seat, yet again he was involved in history changing events, this is bigger than huge and there is no telling what effect it will have on Russia when the truths are brought to the public's knowledge, to the whole world for that matter.

Tim sighed inwardly at the thought of the girls, he remembered Ana so well. She was always a beauty inside and out. Composed at all times although he sensed the fear that engulfed her very being every time she left the safety of the confines of the Royal Palace, she always felt like a moving target. He had lied again to Jack, he had known Anastasia, even communicated with her to help her when the Russian's got too close on the days he would secretly take her out on her own to give her some sense of freedom if only for a few hours, even Verene never knew of the secret trips!

To this day Tim never could understand why the Russians didn't just shoot her when they had the chance, they were quite capable of committing the crime and cleaning up after themselves leaving no trace or any evidence that would lead the government back to them. Perhaps they didn't realise who she was thanks to her disguising herself but they also kept the girls alive in the hope that they may lead them to Anastasia's last resting place, they needed to know for certain she was no longer a threat to the mother country although her daughter and granddaughter were as much a threat as she was.

Verene must have realised how her life was in danger at all times as well as the girls so why didn't the Russians take action towards her?

Why kill Sam now, what information had he got that the Russians didn't want leaked to the public and why did they not want it for themselves, had they just shot themselves in the foot?!

# CHAPTER SIXTEEN

The coughing grew into a choke, the old man struggled to get it under control. His eyes bulged in anger then fear as the help that usually was there within seconds never came. Clutching at his chest with one hand he banged the other on the desktop just as a tall man walked slowly into the doorway silhouetted against the dim light pouring in from the hallway. Thinking help had arrived the old man calmed slightly, once again his eyes big with fear as the mystery man approached, not hurrying, what was that in his hand, a pillow? The old man lifted his head to look up at him just as he shoved the soft mound into his old weathered face contorted with confusion and fear, too weak to fight him off he soon went limp. Silence yet again befell the dark musty room the only sound was the low hissing of the oxygen machine pumping air into the dead man in the wheelchair.

The man walked away out into the hallway, satisfied the job was done, instead of leaving by the backdoor as planned he turned left towards the main doors and let himself out quietly lifting his collar up to hide his face he sprinted down the steps towards the huge gates, showing what looked like a pass he was shown out by one of the guards, out into the cold dawn of another day in this God forsaken country, how he hated it here, his longing for his mother country forever yearning in his soul.

Russia was always in his blood, it had been a while since he had been banished from there for not completing his mission of death. He still had no idea of the importance of the teddy bear but his orders came from the highest office in Russia and he was to find it no matter what or who got in his way.

The old man in the wheelchair had been useful for many many years and now that the bear had been located and lost again the men in charge were tired of his mistakes so he had 'to go' as they say, with his ill health it would be no surprise that he would pass away quietly one dark night, no one would miss him, no one would mourn him.

As the gates crashed shut behind him, the sound of the ancient mechanism locking he heard a shrill scream come from the office as the body of the old man was discovered, he quickened his step and vanished into the early morning foot fall of delivery men making his way into Hyde Park keeping close to the tree lined outer limits for some sort of protection.

# CHAPTER SEVENTEEN

The older woman sat in the window gazing at the beauty of Hyde park, out of habit she was up at the crack of dawn, self preservation would make her rise early in case she had to move location at a second's notice, which she had had to do on many occasions with her mother. She could hear only the dawn chorus, she listened intently as it gave her a sense of freedom the same freedom that the birds of the chorus had. If only life was that simple.

A single red robin landed on her windowsill and stared without song back at the elegant woman as a single tear slowly trickled down her cheek, stopping momentarily to caress the odd wrinkle of which there were very few. Memories passed down to her from her mother of the day's in the house before her life changed forever, before her life on the run.....literally.

When Anastasia and her family were supposedly executed the bodies were piled high in the cellar room where they fell, gunsmoke so thick it was hard to see your own hand in front of you. Anastasia was underneath the bodies, the soldiers failed to check anyone for life after 'finishing' them off with bayonets, not realising Anastasia was well protected by her sisters who had instinctively thrown themselves over her in the hail of bullets knocking her to the floor and unintentional protection from any bullets or bayonet blades.

The soldiers left the family to go outside to celebrate, drinking beer and smoking in the grounds of the house unaware one fragile girl was stronger than expected, as she struggled to move under the weight of her family. Finally freeing herself enough to be able to breath. The soldiers partied well into the night so when it came to collecting the bodies and taking them to their final resting place in the grounds of the elegant house they were not in a fit state to count how many there were, and why would they no one was supposed to have survived?!

A young boy watched in horror as the family were slaughtered mercilessly, the glass in the window so dirty he would not have been seen easily through the smoke of the gunfire. He waited until the soldiers left the room, his only protection was the foliage of a large bush casting more darkness into the room. He watched open mouthed as Anastasia crawled out for breath, the breath of life. He knew he had to do something to help her, he knew who the family were and although his own family had suffered under their rule had never agreed with their impending brutal deaths as it had been predicted what end they would come to although they themselves had no idea, the soldiers were good to them to begin with leaving them to think they were safe in their hands.

He waited in the shade of the bush until darkness fell and the soldiers came for the bodies, thankfully the men were so intoxicated they would never notice any sign of life in Anastasia as she pretended to be dead so as to not raise any suspicion, dumping her body with the others in the makeshift grave in the grounds.

Scurrying from one bush to another he hid close enough to the grave as he possibly could, as the last of the soldiers staggered back to the house not even bothering to cover the bodies with enough dirt the young boy crawled towards Anastasia's twitching hand and took hold of her young cold fingers, instinctively she gripped his hand back. He dragged her out into the cold night air wiping away dirt from her beautiful face out of her eyes and mouth, suddenly cupping her mouth to silence her coughing for fear someone may hear and come running.

It took a few moments for Anastasia to realise she was still alive, clutching to her chest the small golden teddy bear Alexander had given her.

Before panic set in, the boy managed to get her to her knees and scramble to the safety of the bushes where placing a finger to her lips quietly whispered his promise to get her to the safety of his home.

Within half an hour she was sat in his parents rundown excuse for a home, his mother and father sat opposite totally stunned at who was sat shaking in shock in front of their small but much appreciated fire.

It was soon agreed that not only for Anastasia's safety but also for theirs they had to get her as far away as possible. The eldest son was woken and ordered to get dressed, Anastasia was changed into rags, there was no way she could travel anywhere in the expensive attire she was used to. Her hair was roughed up to match the clothes the mother gave her for the long journey ahead.

With enough food and drink to last the long day's they would be traveling the son took Anastasia out of the back of the house towards the barn where the family horse and cart were kept. For the first couple of hours she spent the journey hidden under rags and bales of hay for safety. When the young man decided it was safe he let her sit beside him, she breathed in the smell of the early morning sunshine, the smell of freedom which hung heavy with grief and fear of what the future may hold and the loss her heart would carry for the rest of her life, the loss of her family and country. Little did she know at this point the country that she loved was behind the tragedy.

He managed to get her to a station far enough away from the capital that would be safe for her to get a train to the border.

Before it reached that border however a family member would be waiting to take her off the train to avoid soldiers checking passengers' papers.

Although no one would be looking for her as such if you haven't got identity papers you would end up in jail and they would soon find out who she really was, her fear would give way to revealing her true identity.

After a grateful goodbye Anastasia was taken on yet another horse and cart for an even longer journey. Over the border as far up as possible and into Finland then down to Denmark, across to Holland, Belgium finally into Paris, after so much countryside it was a shock to see the beautiful buildings of the capital city.

Once there Anastasia was left with a distant family member of her mother's who had been ostracized by the Russian government years before. Yet another goodbye to the man and woman who had travelled with her as guides and protectors, finally some sort of relief could be felt but for how long?

Back at the house, the final resting place of the last Tsar and Tsarina of Russia no one noticed the body of Anastasia was no longer by the side of her family, everyone was left to rot, the final insult to a once loved Royal family fallen from grace and favour.

For the next few years Anastasia lived a quiet life of relative luxurious solitude, for fear of being found out it was at least five years until she started to go out in public and socialise amongst the wealthy Parisian people.

Changing her appearance from the recognisable long hair she dyed it darker and wore it up. It wasn't long until she met and fell in love with Louis, he was never told of her real identity, for his safety as much as Anastasia's, and although she loved him deeply she was never really brave enough to tell him.

Her life of normality was short lived, about six months after the deaths of her family a 'loyal' servant had found their way to her with the promise of family jewels being saved and brought to her. Although pleased to see her maid she was suspicious that it was a trap arranged by the Russians. She became her personal maid for many years until one day she disappeared.......with the golden teddy bear. Ana was devastated but also terrified that her fear's proven and her cover blown and the Russians would finally find her after all these years of hiding. She had to come clean to her husband (a multi millionaire) who to her relief admitted he had guessed years ago who she was.

He was a well travelled man and hired a young man called Sam Duggan to locate the bear but also to protect his wife and now their daughter Ana.

Although knowing the Russians would never be far away and probably had been near all along, Anastasia still partied with the nobility and government for years including Russians, if only those same Russians had known who they had been admiring all those years. Now that the bear was gone their cover was in danger, plans were made to escape to England as soon as possible to live with her grandmothers family, the British Royal family, but her husband Louis was murdered one night in a parisian park whilst meeting Sam in the woods thinking they would be safe from anyone over hearing their plans, Louis dead Sam was kidnapped and tortured for days until they decided that he either knew nothing of importance or would never divulge the information if he did. It was decided that letting him go in time he would lead them to Anastasia, he had to have some sort of contact with her.

As she turned and gazed at the robin again something outside caught her eye, movement.

A lot of movement, it was as if the park was swarming with Russians running like frightened scattering beetles, she was confused as to why they were running away from Kensington Palace, away from their target, her. It was alarming as to how many men had actually been hiding in the undergrowth. The once lush green grass of the park was now a sea of men in black.

She stood with both palms on the cold glass watching as they ran towards waiting cars, she almost lost her balance as one man stopped and turned to look up at her he made the sign of slitting his throat with his finger, it was an out and out threat towards her. They knew, the Russians knew she was here and who she was. Slumping back into a chair she knew it was time to move on, now, even here she was no longer safe, she was old, too old to run anymore.

Calling to her maid she instructed her to call Sam he would know what to do next, where to go and what new identity her and her daughter would carry.

The maid came running back in the look of fear etched across her face.

"There was no answer ma'am it's not like him not to answer, do you think something is wrong?"

Ana turned from the window a pained expression on her face, it was all falling apart so quickly, too quickly. She needed Sam here now he always made her feel safe. The two women stood in silence just staring at each other, both nearly jumped out of their skins when the phone rang.

"Ms Romanov?" Ana almost dropped the phone at the sound of the family name. Fear set in even more, she needed to leave NOW.

"Ms Romanov you're safe, please believe me, my name is Jack Courage I work for MI5 on behalf of my aunt, Verene.......and Tim The London Taxi"

At the recognition of Verene and Tim being mentioned and with a hint of a Russian accent Ana whispered.

"But she is no longer with us, who are you really?"

"Please you have to believe me, I need to see you now, Sam was murdered last night. We haven't much time, the Russians are not far behind and are closing in on your real identity."

"Sam, no no he cannot be dead he........he isn't answering his phone, oh poor poor Sam." Ana sighed, no more tears, she had shed so many over the years she thought it was physically impossible to shed any more. A single tear did however fall in honour of her friend, the one man in her life she could rely on since Louis and now he too was gone. Could this man Jack be as reliable? She wasn't sure but at the moment with the Russians so close she had to find someone to help her and Alexandria to escape again into the darkness of anonymity, but where would they go now that was safe?

"Miss Romanov please I need to see you now, it is vital that we protect you and your daughter from the Russians."

Ana nodded at her maid as if to say let him in when he arrives.

"When can you get here Mr Courage?"

"One second......I'm outside now"

"Oh!"

The maid turned on her heal without having to be told, and rushed down to the entrance where she let in a very impatient Jack, who without waiting on ceremony rushed up the stairs two at a time towards where he presumed Ana would be waiting to greet him, eventually he found the right room and walked in to find the most elegant regal woman standing before him, it was as if he had been transported back to the time of the Romanov family, so like her mother it was eerie. Instinctively he bowed, low. Well she was Royalty after all.

If he hadn't known who she really was he would have guessed straight away she was of Romanov descent, she was the spitting image of The Anastasia down to the hair style and features, obviously when out and about she made the effort not to look too like her true self, the russians would know straight away who she was related to and her life would be over.

He explained what happened to Sam, barely any emotion crossed her beautiful features, but her knuckles went white, total control.

Jack left the palace after overseeing the new security measures, even though the Russians had now left their posts outside he was not taking any chances with the women's safety. At least three groups of ten more men were stationed around the palace.

The hum of drones flying overhead in the park signified to Jack and Tim MI5 were up to speed, and sending all information they were recording to Tim's inbuilt system as well as headquarters.

# CHAPTER EIGHTEEN

Tim sat and watched as in the distance men in black clothing were literally appearing from nowhere and running, probably back to the embassy but why? Why leave their target unattended now, they had killed Sam, failed in getting the bear but the one woman they had been after for so long was here and although protected by Royal guards and MI5 she was the one person they wanted along with her daughter.

Something was wrong, he radiod through to Chief Gibson who informed him of the sudden death of Vadim Yurovsky at the Russian embassy, there were no suspicious circumstances as he had been old and ill for some time but something didn't feel right so the Chief wanted Tim on it while Jack looked after Ana and her daughter.

Tim called through to Jack and relayed the conversation he had had with the Chief and said he would be back as soon as he had spoken to Boris at the embassy.

Speeding off into the warmth of the new morning sunshine he made his way through the city traffic until he came to the large imposing crumbling embassy. Parking round the back where he met Boris before as he radioed through to his Russian friend.

"Boris it's Tim we need to meet NOW!!"

"Tim, all ell has as you english say 'broken lose' here, Mr Yurovsky is dead, he was a very important man in old regime."

"I know but was it murder did someone kill him Boris I need to know everything that happened last night. Can you find out for me?"

"Of course, of course Comrade I will do my best." With that he was off running through the dark passages of the embassy until he came to the hallway with the black and white tiled floor only this time it was full of men in black suits. Everyone was talking in hushed voices, one man in particular Maxim, the head of security, seemed to be having a private conversation with a female nurse in the corner of the hallway, nothing out of the ordinary there but Boris noticed he had hold of her wrist in a vice like grip and by the look of fear and pain on her face it must hurt. Boris scurried as fast and as carefully as he could towards the couple so he could listen in on their conversation, running between black covered legs almost being trodden on a few times as he squeezed through, he really needed to lose some weight.

"He told me to wait five minutes in my office while he dealt with him, it was awful I could hear him choking, then all of a sudden the choking stopped. I went into the Comrade's office after the five minutes and that's when I found him, dead."

"Where was the man at this point?" The man tightened his grip on the young woman's wrist making her wince in pain. You cannot lie to these people especially not in here, they will always find a way to get the truth, and you have nowhere to run!

"I didn't see him again Sir……..although I did hear the front door click as I walked past into the office but at the time thought nothing of it."

"Good, good." His grip momentarily tightened as he realised that the killer had left the building straight after the murder, he loosened his hand as he heard the girl let out a small cry.

"Prosti" (sorry) he let go of her, motioned for her to run along as he pondered his next move. Scanning the room he noticed the two men stood in a corner staring at him, waiting for their next orders. He flicked his head for them to meet him in the room opposite the office where Yurovsky had died. He waited in there for the men to join him, it contained a large conference table and chairs, the flag of his mother country hung over the ornate fireplace, instinctively he bowed his head fractionally in respect for his Russia, oh how he wished he was back there now. He had had enough of this pathetic place, England, the people were too soft there was no political structure that made it's countries men do as they should, no strength no fear of reprisals.

The two men walked in and shut the door behind them, no one else must be privy to this conversation, although why they were in the conference room was a risk in itself as everyone knew it was always bugged by the regime.

"I take it everything is in order for the catering?" Code for all tracks covered. You can't be too careful in any room in this building, it was not just this one that would be bugged. He stood facing the fireplace, his back to the two men who exchanged questioning looks.

"I think we should change suppliers, I am not happy with the service, it's time to move on to another company." Code for, our job is done and it's time to get the hell out of here before anyone realises we are involved!!

"Yes sir, we will organise the paper work straight away." Passports and identity papers and tickets back to Russia, home at last. It had been a while since he had seen his own family, he hoped they were alive and well, he had not been able to keep in touch with them for fear of endangering their lives. No one escaped the rules of the regime whether you worked for them or not you still had to go by the rules, their rules.

Silence indicated to the two men that the meeting was over and it was time to leave him. They left quietly, shutting the door behind them. As it clicked shut a deep voice wafted from the dark corner beside the door, he hadn't noticed someone sat in the high backed chair in the shadows.

He flinched at the sudden intrusion on his short lived rejoicing at going home.

"So your catering business is still going strong Comrade, tut tut. I thought you would have learned a new cuisine by now." Maxim paled in fear at the recognition of the voice in the darkness, he knew that he would never see his mother country again or his family, dam he thought he had had every angle covered. It took a few seconds to piece together what happened next as the doors opened the same time as the bullet hit him in the chest, he looked from the darkened doorway to the blood seeping through his crisp white shirt slowly spreading outwards, to the barrel of the silencer in the corner of the room. Slowly he slumped to the floor not quite landing as the two men that were in here earlier caught him as he dropped to his knees, the look of realisation on his face as it dawned on him he had been double crossed by his own comrades. Darkness came as his life ebbed away, they dragged his body to the chair opposite the man in the corner, dumping him onto the crimson red leather, the same crimson that slowly seeped across his shirt..

"Leave us now, you can dispose of him later, lock the door on the way out we don't want to be disturbed do we?"

The two men did as they were instructed and left Maxim slumped dead in the chair opposite the man as he lit a cigarette, another job well done.

As the two men left the room, Andrei, the tall one scanned the room making sure no one was taking any notice of their movements as the short fat one Vlad locked the door behind them. Neither of them noticed the young nurse watching from the side of the opulent staircase near the door to the basement. Nervously she rubbed her sore wrist, something was wrong very wrong, where was Maxim she was sure he entered the room before them.

She flinched as she felt something against her ankle, looking down she almost screamed at the sight of a very large rat, the only thing that stopped her was the fact he was dressed in a small but heavy black coat and a Russian fur hat, and had his 'finger' over his lips as if to say keep silent. Momentarily dumbstruck silence came easily.

"Follow me quickly, it may just save your life." With that he scurried off towards the door to the basement, Darya followed him without question once he had mentioned saving her life. Whether working in the mother country or the embassy your life was never your own or safe.

The door closed behind her as she entered, panic set in as all went dark. A single flame whooshed into life lighting the corridor enough for her to see the same rat holding a candle and the silhouettes of more rats. Frozen to the spot Darya hadn't realised at first that another rat had gently grabbed the hem of her uniform and soon began to lead her to the back door. The shadows of her rescuers flickered along the walls in the candle light, like ghosts of the night, no one said a word as she followed asking no questions.

They reached the back door leading to the bin area, one of the rats opened the door carefully in case anyone was outside, the old door creaked loudly, everyone stopped, no one dared to breathe in case even their breath was too loud.

After checking outside Boris motioned for Darya to follow him outside quietly. The coldness of the morning still hung in the air which engulfed her in more fear, she only had on a short sleeved nurses uniform. Just as she was beginning to shake due to the cold a small voice whispered from behind a bin.

"Pst pst over here quickly." Darya turned but couldn't see anyone, just as she was about to think she was imagining the voice Robbie popped out, almost frightening her half to death!

"Come on follow me, thanks Boris catch you later." Robbie grabbed her hand and half dragged her towards the gate which was almost hidden due to overgrown bushes, this was to their advantage as it cast some large shadows for them to hide in while

Robbie attempted to open the rotting old wooden structure. It wasn't long until the gate was open, a gust of wind washed over her as if the freedom it offered was in the cold air engulfing her. Waiting at the curb was Tim door wide open, Robbie grabbed Darya's hand and half dragged her again but this time towards the open door, a single gunshot could be heard whizzing past her head as Robbie literally pushed her into Tim following closely behind as the door slammed shut and Tim shot off into the traffic with such speed that neither Robbie or Darya could physically get up off the floor of the taxi until he managed to slow down to a normal pace. Bullets ricocheted off Tim's metal work, which was thankfully bullet proof. A frightened Darya lay on the floor with her hands and arms over her head in some sort of protection, fear gripping her, memories of her motherland regime, the same fear from her childhood hiding from Russian bullets.

"It's ok, it's ok Tim is bulletproof." Robbie touched her arm in an attempt to calm her but she recoiled in horror into the corner of the cab, not quite sure what to make of a talking rat and a bulletproof taxi.

"Hi I'm Tim, your carriage to safety. Please take a seat you are quite safe inside of me. I will take you somewhere where no one can get to you"

This was getting stranger by the second, a talking rat who was also clothed like a human and a talking taxi. Darya didn't quite know whether to laugh or cry. Scrambling up onto the seat she noticed out of the back window the embassy getting smaller and smaller, a coldness snaked down her spine, she had never been able to leave the confinement of the embassy before. If she had ever wanted to (which she did but just never had a viable reason to) she would have to have written permission.

Some sort of relief then washed over her at the thought of freedom, she relaxed into the seat, closed her eyes then they shot open at the loud bang outside of the cab.

"I do apologise madam but it was only a car backfiring nothing for you to worry about" Tim noticed her relax again although still on edge to a point.

Arriving at the mews Tim was surprised that there were no men in black waiting for them, however with the comotion earlier at the death of Vadim Yurovsky and the mass exodus of men he thought it probably had something to do with that.

The door and shutters shot down with such a bang that Darya almost shot out of her skin again, Jack was there this time to let her out of Tim and offer his hand which after initial hesitation she took hold of.

The look of confusion as she saw the plasma screen with all the pictures of people some she recognised was Jack's cue to explain why she was here.

"Miss Popov welcome, my name is Jack Courage of MI5 I work for the British Government. I am working on a case involving The Romanov family."

At the mention of the Russian Royal's name and the fact this stranger knew her full name Darya paled and leant on the arm of the sofa to steady herself. Had she just jumped out of the frying pan into the fire by leaving the embassy? Either way her life was in danger, she instinctively looked around for an escape route, a moan escaped her lips at the realisation that there was none. It took a few minutes for her to realise that Jack had put a calming hand on her arm, her terrified eyes locked with his as he looked at her with pity. He knew only too well what would happen to her should the Russian's find her, he needed to get her to Chief Gibson at head office as soon as possible and in one piece.

Darya's eyes widened as she caught sight of who was on the large screen, she looked from the pictures then to Jack questionaly. Slowly she moved closer, her hands shaking from fear tenderly moved pictures and papers around that were laid out on the table below the screen. Her hand hovered over a photograph of Ana and Alexandria, her face shot round to look at Jack more fear in her eyes, her hand resting on the photograph.

"They are in danger Sir, my people will stop at nothing to make sure their secrets are never told. Where are they now?"

Jack hesitated, although he was sure she wouldn't want to go back to the embassy he knew he could not divulge any information on the women for fear that if Darya was caught and taken back she may very well tell them everything.

He needed to get her to headquarters quickly, Tim sensing his plan opened his side door again as Jack motioned for her to get back in. He got in the driver's seat, within minutes they were all on their way along the cobbled mews street.

Darya gasped as she locked eyes with a tall Russian as he stared back at her, her palms against the cold of the glass window, a coldness filled her whole being along with the fear that life had now become very very dangerous. Sitting back in her seat she was resigned to the fact no matter what she did now her life would never be the same again……if she actually survived.

Of course Tim had seen the Russian as well as had Jack.

"They can't hurt you now Darya." Jack's words fell silent on deaf ears, gripped with fear she heard nothing, just silence as if impending death was the only option now.

Travelling through the heavy London traffic Darya sat open mouthed at the glorious architecture of the city. When she had arrived in the country a couple of years ago she was taken straight to the embassy and never saw the wonderful sights of the city again.

She had never even seen the wonders of Moscow, her own capital of The Mother Country. Luckily it was a lovely day and the sun shone on the tall buildings reflecting light off the buildings like comforting angels sent to protect her.

Tim drove in and out of cars and vans heading for the MI5 headquarters near the Thames.

He knew he had to get her to safety as soon as possible, especially now that at least one Russian had been spotted, he and Jack knew these men were everywhere and not always hiding the fact.

"Miss Popov we will be arriving shortly at the headquarters of MI5 and you will be safe there. Jack will take you up to meet with Chief Gibson who will ask you a few questions. Please don't worry."

Darya sat back in her seat, the excitement of a new city now gone at the thought of having to go into another secure building, one of which she knew nothing about, was it even safe? Fear gripped her chest like a vice, even more so when Tim drove up to the basement entrance and the large garage door lifted to allow them entry. She turned in her seat to watch as the door closed behind them, shutting them off from the outside world literally, with all the technology in here no one would hear a single word anyone said, no one would hear her scream.....help would never come should she need it from her fellow Russians.

Tim drove up the main ramp into what looked like a huge garage filled with all sorts of cars, vehicles used for missions, everyday use and workers transport. Nothing out of the ordinary really just another garage. He parked near a doorway, two men stepped out of the shadows startling Darya, one opened the door to let her out while the other one approached her with a body scanner to make sure she wasn't armed, all clear.

Jack got out of the driving seat and walked round to join her as Tim moved slowly away to a parking space where he could wait for the two of them while they had their meeting with The Chief.

The two of them followed the silent man up the stairs, dimly lit by warm yellow downlights casting haunting shadows along the way.

Darya didn't feel any warmth from what little light shone, in fact she shook from nerves more than the coldness of fear that engulfed her.

Jack gently touched her arm reassuringly making her flinch out of her own little world of fear. He smiled as if to say 'don't worry' she nodded but as she walked along the endless corridor she felt as if she was walking slowly to the gallows.

It wasn't long until they came to a door which creaked on opening, the sound seemed to echo along the narrow never ending corridor. It was even darker than the last corridor, the small wall lights cast long dagger-like shadows as they automatically flicked on as they strolled past them to the large door at the end.

As they reached the final door Darya looked at Jack as if to say 'is this it, is this the end?' there seemed to be no way out now, the end of the corridor, the end of the line! The end of her life!

Jack looked at her reassuringly and placed a hand on her shaking shoulder.

"It's fine Darya go on in." With that the door was opened from the inside by a tall woman in black, hair scraped back, dark rimmed glasses no smile no welcome. The angel of death?

# CHAPTER NINETEEN

The Chief waited in his office for Jack and Darya to join him, he wasn't quite sure what had happened but this woman could be useful in the case, someone on the inside now on the outside and in fear for her life. The Russian's will stop at nothing to get to her before she spills the beans, so time was of the essence in getting her to a safe place. The future for her should she survive will be a new identity, new location….. survival!

A knock at the door brought the Chief out of his deep thoughts, turning from the window he saw Jack and Darya enter his office. She was quite young but wore an old fashioned nurse's uniform making her look like someone from the history books of old Russia. He motioned for them to sit, no one spoke until they were all seated. The woman in black nodded at the Chief before leaving, Darya noted the nod, was this it, the secret sign to end her life?

"Chief, Darya Popov was a nurse to Vadim Yurovsky but she tells me there was also a male nurse that was above her that also looked after him, he was the last person to see him alive. She believes he had a hand in his death. He disappeared the night Yurovsky died and hasn't been seen since."

The chief sat pondering this latest bit of information. Vadim Yurovsky was the elderly son of Yakov Yurovsky who was in charge of the soldiers guarding the Russian Royal family when they were held in Ipatiev house and presided over their execution. After the cold war and deaths he disappeared and was never heard of again, people presumed he was either dead or being paid to keep quiet whilst in exile.

Vadim was born sometime after Yakov was involved in the historical atrocity but when his father learned of the possible survival of Anastasia he made it his mission to find her and dispose of her fearing she would blow his cover and own safety.

He despised her family and everything they had stood for and took great delight in being the one that brought the family down. When Yakov Yurovsky died his son Vadim made it his life's work to carry on his father's mission, he was convinced that his father's death had not been due to natural causes. Over the years he was determined to avenge his father's demise and find any trace of Anastasia. As the years passed his health declined to such an extent he was confined to a wheelchair and his breathing had to be aided by oxygen tanks on the back. This however did not stop him on his journey looking for Anastasia or smoking very strong Russian cigarettes.

Darya sat with her hands clenched in her lap, not sure if she was safe or not with these people. How would she know if she was actually in the headquarters of MI5, she had never been allowed out of the embassy.

The chief and Jack sat talking, she managed to keep up with most of what they were discussing but being kept in the dark regarding who lived and worked in the embassy didn't help her much at the moment, she had just got on with her job, you never asked questions.

Jack turned to her and asked "Who was the main man you had to answer to in the embassy, Yurovsky?"

Darya shifted in her seat, uncomfortable at the simple question. She looked from one man to the other and back again.

"Maxim, but er I think something might have happened to him."

"What makes you say that?" The chief leant forward in his seat, hands clasped in anticipation.

"He had a meeting in the conference room with two of his men, he always seemed to be in quiet conversations with them, this particular time late last night he went into the conference room with them but never came out. The two men left locking the door behind them but Maxim never left the room."

Jack looked at the Chief, they needed to find out who this Maxim is and what happened to him, Boris was their only man on the inside. Tim was listening in on the conversation and took it upon himself to return to the embassy to talk to Boris.

He drove slowly through the garage and towards the exit door where a silent young man flipped the switch to open the door and let him out, no nod of acknowledgement, in this job 'you were never there'.

He drove out into the busy city traffic once more, just another black taxi amongst hundreds of others, but they all knew who he was, all the London transport knew who he was and in times of need they were always on hand to help wherever they could.

Tim drove right back to the embassy and Boris, his Russian friend was waiting for him which Tim found odd although handy as he wouldn't have to hang around long waiting for him. To Tim's surprise Boris and about twenty of his men ran up to him and jumped into the back, Boris shouting...

"Drive drive drive.....I've av always wanted to shout that...... but honestly Tim we need to get out of here now before anyone sees us.!"

Tim didn't stop to ask questions, not because he trusted Boris, it was the hail of bullets that got him moving.

Small bits of metal pinged off his armour plated bodywork sending sparks flying all over the place. Fellow taxis seeing him gaining on them at speed and the bullets flying behind him, moved out of his way to let him through then closed the gap behind him so that anyone trying to chase him wouldn't be able to get to him, giving him a head start.

Route masters ahead of him moved to either side of the road so he could speed off into the distance and make his way back to MI5 headquarters. Dipping in and out of traffic his passengers had difficulty staying in their seats. Boris hung onto the side handle as if his life depended on it and at this moment it actually did. The other rats rolled around on the floor unable to get a grip on anything, bumping into each other and the doors, the odd ouch could be heard over screeching tyres, Tim's tyres. Cyclists shouted obscenities as they were almost knocked off their bikes, pedestrians crossing the road threw themselves backwards to avoid being hit by Tim who tried his best to miss everyone.

Tim radioed through to Jack as he drove through the city streets.

"Jack, Jack, may day may day Jack get down stairs NOW!!!"

There was no panic in Tim's voice, only urgency, the Russians knew something was wrong and had started to react.....badly. As Tim arrived back at the MI5 garage door he screeched around the last corner at speed almost hitting the top of his taxi sign on the bottom of the door as it rose out of his way....just. The two men on the other side threw themselves out of the way landing on the floor winded and sore.

Tim didn't slow down inside like before, he raced towards the door where he had left Jack earlier, his friend wasn't there, he came to a screeching stop just as Jack shot out of the door at such a speed he landed on Tim's bonnet.

He looked through Tim's windscreen and was shocked to see the back of the cab full to the brim with rat's, Russian rat's looking very dishevelled and bruised!! In the middle of the pack of rat's was a large rodent, dressed in full Russian regalia. Jack slid off of Tim's bonnet and lunged for the door opening it, as he did so a pile of bodies fell out onto the ground.

Jack leant down to help Boris to his feet.

"Maxim's body was found this morning in one of the green bins amongst the shredded documents, he ad been shot Sir." Boris did the sign of the cross on his chest in respect for the dead. One small rat pretended to be shot stuck his tongue out as he 'died' and clutching his chest fell to the fall as if dead, some of the others laughed quietly like naughty children.

Tim tutted at the rats and opened the driver's door and shouted at his partner to get in.

"Jack get in please we need to go to the embassy now, Boris you're coming with us we need you to get Jack and Robbie in safely."

Boris's eyes bulged with fear and disbelief then suddenly excitement at the thought of the fight ahead, fighting the old regime.

Dragging the 'dead' rat to his feet who momentarily hung like a corpse as Boris announced that they would all join Jack in the fight against their countrymen, much to the annoyance of the other rats, who shrugged and got back into Tim's cab, this time some of them used the seat belts, strapping themselves in, the others sat on each other's laps for safety!!

Tim revved his engine, the smell of burning rubber filled the air as he turned himself almost on the spot, the two men at the garage door stood stock still goggle eyed as he headed for them again, throwing themselves out of the way just in time as he left the building.

The Chief running behind waving some paperwork at him, Tim turned again leaving more tyre marks on the road surface in the process, driving past the Chief Jack grabbed the search warrant without Tim even stopping to see if the ink was dry on the paper.

"Oh hell this isn't going to go well." The Chief ran his fingers through his white hair in sheer frustration but deep down he knew he had the best man and machine on the job.

Legally a search warrant wasn't worth the paper it was printed on and had no jurisdiction in the embassy due to diplomatic immunity, but The Chief knew Jack wouldn't be going in via the correct political or legal channels but it always paid to have a paper trail.

# CHAPTER TWENTY

Tim raced into the lunchtime traffic again, and screeched to a standstill. Grid lock, this time it was so busy not even his fellow taxis and cars could move out of the way for him, revving his engine he reversed slightly then without hesitation mounted the pavement on the left hand side of the road much to the alarm of the rat's in the back of him who all grimaced in anticipation of either a crash or getting arrested, covering their eyes.

Speeding along the path pedestrians scattered to avoid being run over, one man fell into the road right in front of a route master bus who luckily was a mate of Tim's and had stopped just in time, his bumper brushing the top of the man's head!

Jack had his hands on the steering wheel but was just going through the motions as Tim was well in control of the situation, although as much as Jack trusted Tim he did cover his eyes on one occasion as they just narrowly missed a woman and pushchair.

Eventually Tim found a break in the traffic and rejoined the flow, this time on the road, Boris and his men breathed a sigh of relief which sadly didn't last long when they realised they were very close to the embassy.

Tim had to stop again, they could only get so close as the surrounding roads were clogged by black cars with blacked out glass, Russians! Jack scanned the area and made the executive decision that there was no way that Tim would be able to physically get any closer so it was now down to Boris and his men to go back into the embassy and see what they can find out.

Within minutes Boris and his men were out on the pavement, the small rats standing to attention awaiting their next orders.

They didn't have to wait long, the plan was for them all to sneak back into the embassy and have a good look around then report back to Jack and Tim as to who was in there and what they were doing.

Running close to the wall for protection they made their way to the back gate, stopping abruptly they found that that was a no go, Maxim's body was just being put into a coffin, there were Russians everywhere, Boris backed up bumping into some of his men who were not quick enough to move. Turning on their heels they ran round towards the old wooden gate and crept through without being seen……or so they thought.

A lone Russian was standing in the shadow's watching, smoking a Russian cigarette, dropping the last of it to the floor. He slowly crushed it under foot then walked away through the gate and towards the bin area, he stopped and watched as the body was removed then entered the building through the back door by the bins. The men around all stood to attention, who was this man? Boris didn't recognise him, although he was sure he had seen him somewhere before but not here at the embassy and he would know as he had lived here for a while.

Boris took a mental note of what the man was like to relay to Tim when he got back to him, his men rushing around him, scurrying in and out of the bins looking for clues, finding nothing of importance, actually they found nothing at all, not even a drop of blood. Just like before the smell of bleach indicated a thorough clean up.

As the man exited the building again he walked through the old gate, he turned and locked eyes with Boris, sending shivers down the rat's spine, the man grinned knowingly at him as if to say 'you won't find anything to pin on me' and as quick as a flash he was gone into the city once more.

Boris was frozen to the spot deep in thought when one of his men rushed up to him grabbing his arm and dragging him towards the back door to the basement.

"We've got something Sir please hurry." Boris snapped out of his trance and hurried behind his fellow rat wondering what on earth they could have found that had him so excited.

"A visa in the name of the dead gentleman Sir, he was supposed to be going home to Russia."

"Who stopped him and why?" Boris pondered the information, folding the visa into a small parcel so that it would fit into his pocket to show Tim later. Why would someone kill him when he was leaving the country anyway, what had he done wrong to deserve to die? Before he could answer his own questions he was dragged into the basement, into the dimly lit passageway he knew only too well and hated just as much.

They scurried along the wooden floor the sound of claws tip tapping as they did so, making their way to the main entrance hall they stopped in their tracks at the amount of men in black suits that filled the black and white tiled room.

There was barely any room to move. It was so full, they pushed their way towards the front door, some men tried to look down at what or who was pushing past them but couldn't get a good enough look. This was to Boris's and his men's advantage as they reached the office door where the old man in the wheelchair used to reside, they all pushed together at the door opening it just enough so that they could squeeze in. There were no lights on and it was empty, totally empty.

All the furniture was gone, the ornate desk was no longer standing proud in the middle of the room, nothing except for one thing that seemed odd to Boris, the wheelchair, it was covered in a stained sheet and there seemed to be something underneath.

Boris moved closer, slowly, reaching for the sheet with his right hand he took hold of one corner and pulled it away. The room filled with loud gasps as the removal of the sheet revealed a body, the body of the old man, his face contorted in agony, the final agony as his life ebbed away.

Dropping the sheet in shock Boris almost threw up, he had seen some horrors over the years living here in the embassy but this really beat them all into a cocked hat. He slowly began to walk away backwards still looking at the old man's face, a face that will never leave his mind for a long time. One of his men who also couldn't take his eyes off the body grabbed his arm and whispered to him...

"Sir, Sir we need to get out of here before we are caught. Please Sir."

"I er think, er this is odd, I don't understand why they would leave his body here." Flies began to buzz louder and louder as they filled the air, the body had started to decompose, the smell hung heavy in the air, the shock of seeing the body had momentarily blocked their sense of smell, when it was unblocked they all began to gag and run for the door only to find it shut. Panic set in as the only way of opening it was to pull which would prove difficult even impossible for the rats as the handle was too high for them to reach without standing on each other's shoulders, and at this point they were too shaken to think straight enough to perform such a feat. Plus one of the rats noticed a draft coming from an open window and motioned to Boris that it would be easier to get out of there rather than attempt to open the door and enter the packed entrance hall.

The men soon began to form a tower so that they could exit through the open window and out into the grounds and hopefully to some sort of safety. Two of the last men dangled a third one so that he could help Boris up, with him being quite chunky it was a struggle but eventually they managed to get him onto the windowsill, he lay flat on his stomach out of breath. He soon found the strength to get out of the window when the door shot open and two men rushed in. The rats landed in a heap on the floor, looking up towards the window they screamed as the approaching body of Boris came hurtling towards them, landing with a thud on top of the pile. No one said a word, no one was capable of saying anything other than URGH!!!!

After a few minutes the rats managed to get up, brushing themselves down they started to run back around towards the bin area, from there they made their way towards the old back gate, thankfully it was left ajar. Pulling on it they made their way onto the outside pavement and Tim.

Boris banged on his door to be let in, Jack was nowhere to be seen which surprised him. Tim opened the door and everyone got in.

"Tim I don't understand what is going on, but the old man in the wheelchair is still in his office, in his chair under a dirty sheet and every bit of furniture has been removed from the room, apart from the chair and the body the room is completely empty."

"Why would they keep a rotting body in the room? Anything else?"

Boris explained the amount of men that were rammed into the entrance hall, they both came to the conclusion that all of the men they had witnessed leaving the grounds of Kensington Palace had now congregated in the embassy probably awaiting their next instructions.

The embassy was now full of Russian agents, how many no one knew but it must be a hell of a lot to fill the embassy hallway, thirty, fifty maybe more!!

"Where's Jack Tim?" Boris gazed back at the embassy, his mouth fell open when he saw Jack running.......along the roof and following behind was a fellow rat in a denim jacket and red baseball hat.....Robbie!!!!!!

"Don't worry about Jack, he's got it all covered, not too sure what his plan is yet but I'm sure he will come up with something......soon....I hope!"

# CHAPTER TWENTY ONE

Jack and Robbie ran alongside the embassy looking for a way in without being seen or setting off any security. They noticed a man in black coming out of the old gate way. Robbie stopped momentarily to stare at him, he seemed more rougher round the edges unlike all the other men who were dressed the same but sharper, this man had long hair tied back in a ponytail and facial hair and to be frank he looked dirty!!! Robbie shivered as their eyes locked, the scruffy man not once missing a step, he still didn't take his eyes off of Robbie as he pushed the old gate and vanished.

Robbie chased after Jack to tell him what he had just seen but Jack was too busy trying to find a way in so he decided to leave it until later.

Knowing Boris, he and his men would be nearby behind the gate they had decided it would be safer to find another way in. About two hundred yards along they found a part of the wall had crumbled to such an extent due to lack of care over the years that they could actually squeeze through the gap. Broken masonry underfoot crunched loudly, stopping them momentarily in case anyone had heard them. When they decided it was safe to carry on they made their way towards the back of the main building, this time way behind the bin area, this must be part of the original building that was no longer in use, it was even more decrepit than the main building, almost a ruin. On the main back wall was a rusting ladder that hung precariously against it, a few fittings looked too rusty to hold it up and some were missing but the two of them decided it was the only way in, by climbing up the ladder they could get to the roof and enter the embassy that way.

Jack went first and Robbie followed slowly behind him, he was in his element, another mission with his friend. For a rat he was very excitable at times but damn good at his job.

As Jack pulled himself up towards the top of the building his foot slipped, a couple of screws rusty from years of rain fell out of the wall hitting Robbie on the head as they plummeted to the ground, thankfully neither Jack or Robbie followed them.

After pausing for a few seconds Jack carried on climbing as did Robbie. Jack turned as he stood on the top of the roof and helped Robbie up over the edge. The view of the city was amazing from up here, they could see for miles and miles, they could also see how vast the embassy grounds were, old and new, actually old and very old. The oldest bit was more derelict than the newer bit, there seemed to be some movement down there, why would anyone be walking amongst so much rubble? Jack strained his eyes a bit more on two men picking their way through the broken buildings heading away from the main building, one tall and thin the other short and fat. He recognised them from the auction house and the toy store. He watched as they approached a small building and entered through a metal door. The door looked new, it must be a secret room, a bunker? It looked more like a shed with a very strong door, there had to be more to it than those four small walls.

"Those are the two guy's we keep seeing Jack, they taking up gardening or something.......what the?" As the boy's were watching the two men the heavy metal door suddenly opened and to their amazement a stream of men in black suits started to march out one by one, the procession seemed to go on and on and on. Ricky lost count at forty men and they were still leaving the 'garden shed'.

"We need to get a look inside that 'shed'." Robbie rolled his eyes, it had taken them long enough to get up here onto the roof and he didn't really fancy going back down that ladder again, to be honest he didn't think it would hold their weight a second time.

Jack had a look around the rooftop to see if there was anything out of place or out of the ordinary. There were the usual communications systems, all very high tech, even some that Jack had never seen before even in his job. He reached into his rucksack and took out a small box which looked like a transmitter, it had a small screen and about twenty buttons and a keypad. Keying in a long code he waited whilst it beeped away tracking the airwaves around them. His eyes grew bigger when the information slowly came up on the screen, the Russians had somehow managed to bypass all of MI5's technical blocking of radar's and phone signals. They could actually hear conversations from inside MI5 headquarters, how in heaven's name did they get through that system of high tech security?

"We've got a problem Robbie, if they can hear everything from headquarters then we can't communicate with anyone there without someone here knowing our every move. Robbie....we're on our own now, hopefully we can talk to Tim, but even he might be compromised."

Robbie slumped to the floor, he loved working with Tim and Jack, he knew he was always safe even in the midst of terrible danger but they always had the backing and support from MI5.....that's when they didn't go rogue!!!

"Jack I can hear you and I've managed to connect to their system and blocked their communication signals so they won't be able to log into our's, it wasn't easy I have no idea what system they are using but it's good, damn good"

"Thanks Tim, Robbie and I are going inside to see if we can find a way of getting into 'the shed' there must be another entrance." Robbie looked at Jack shocked at the thought of going inside the embassy, he thought it would be safer to stay at a distance for a while, he wasn't a coward but on the same level he wasn't that brave.

He noticed a commotion, looking over the edge of the roof he could see that the grounds that were strewn with large bits of rubble and the remains of old buildings was now swarming with men in black suits clambering over the mess and heading for the main building, from where they were situated the men looked like an army of black ants. Robbie suddenly threw himself back onto the floor as one man looked up towards the roof, he hoped he hadn't been seen, he took a peak over the edge just as a bullet ricocheted off the stone work, Jack grabbed the scruff of his jacket and pulled him out of harm's way and still holding onto him made a run for the middle of the rooftop and a small doorway which should lead into an attic room presumably.

Jack tried the door and was amazed to find it unlocked, also suspicious as to why it would be, he let go of Robbie who slipped to the floor but got up as quick as he went down and covered Jack's back.

Peering round the door nothing seemed to be out of the ordinary, it was dark which for this embassy that was not a surprise, there was an odd odour hanging in the air, was it the smell of death?

The two of them slowly made their way into the small attic room, it was full of old furniture, Robbie nudged Jack as he noticed the ornate desk from the old man's office, it must have taken a few men to get that up here it was very heavy looking. Why hide it away anyway?

Jack tried the door which he assumed would lead to a corridor or stairs, trying the handle he was relieved to find it was also unlocked, opening it slowly in case anyone was waiting on the other side he realised there was something or someone lurking in the shadows.

He was sure he could see a set of eyes staring back at him, he was thankful when Robbie shone a light on them to find that it was a very stern looking Russian in a painting.

Relaxing momentarily they began to make their way down the dark corridor by torch light, eventually after trying numerous doors they found one that led to a staircase heading down.

Jack put his foot on the first step and flinched slightly as it creaked due to old age and lack of use. As they made their way down to another corridor they were met by more eyes, every wall was covered in portraits of old leaders of the Mother Country, not one was smiling, Robbie almost walked into the back of Jack as he stared up at the grim faces that stared back at him, he was convinced that their eyes followed them as they carried on walking and walking. The corridor must be the whole length of the building it seemed never ending, the darkness didn't help.

Eventually they came to the end and another door, this one however was locked, it took Jack a while but he managed with his set of skeleton keys to unlock it, he turned the handle very slowly, with all the creaking floor boards he wasn't taking any chances. He found the slower he opened it the more it creaked!! So he swung it open, he felt it hit something, the two of them froze and something slumped to the floor.

Robbie gingerly looked around the door and found to his horror a man in black in a heap and unconscious, a large red mark on his nose and forehead from where the door hit him.

Jack pushed the door more to enable him to get through and the body to move out of the way. They made their way to the top of the next set of steps and walked down to yet another door.

This one was unlocked and led to yet another corridor and another door, Robbie was beginning to think they would never get out, they would be continuously walking down corridors and finding more doors!!

Eventually they felt that they had come downwards enough and sure enough one of the doors opened onto a lighter corridor and they could hear the soft rumble of voices....a lot of voices, Jack signalled for Robbie to stay quiet, Robbie laughed inwardly, the last thing he was going to do was make any sound that would bring the whole of the Russian embassy running towards them.

It was a relief to be in more light but also meant they would be easier to find, they moved towards the end of the opulently decorated corridor, more portraits, more up to date but still very depressing looking. When they reached the end and the door the sound of voices had become louder, Jack took hold of the handle, cold to the touch he turned it slowly and opened it an inch then stared into the room. It was filled to the brim with men in black suits and dark glasses, was this some sort of comic adventure film convention?! He decided to not take any chances and shut the door to come up with a plan. If they retraced their steps they would end up back on the roof and a dodgy ladder, if they go forward they would be right in the middle of the 'Russian army' and certain death.

"Pst...pst Jack over here." A voice from behind and lower down, there was a rat stood by the side of him, where had he come from, they didn't see him when they came along the corridor?

"Follow me." He turned and seemed to grab at something below one of the portrait's, it was a hole in the wall that opened a secret door of which the portrait hung on.

Not waiting to be told twice the two of them entered another room, this one was darker than the corridor with a musty smell of dust and old times. It was full of sofas and chairs, a bit like an old gentlemans club. They followed the rat to another doorway which led to yet another corridor, this one was presumably used by staff as it was bare of decoration and portraits and lighter.

Jack and Robbie followed behind silently down one staircase after another. It wasn't long until they found themselves down in the basement, Robbie recognised it from when he was there before. The rat led them towards the main entrance hall stopping short of entering, turning he put his finger to his lips to signify keeping quiet.

The sound of low voices could be heard wafting into the basement hallway, foreign words lingering like smoke in the air.

Jack spun round as he was tapped on the shoulder, his gun was drawn in automatic defense aimed at……a suit…..he had turned to see a black suit with a rat's head poking out of it, it took a few seconds for him to realise that it was being held up by a tower of rats, the top rat raised his eyebrows as if to say 'put it on' another rat handed him some dark glasses.

Within minutes he was dressed all in black, putting on the dark glasses he was ready to enter the entrance hall as a Russian.

Robbie jumped up and high fived him, Jack paused then walked into the entrance hall with confidence, he didn't want anyone to realise he was an impostor straight away!!

He looked around for any familiar faces, seeing none he squeezed through the throng of seemingly identical men in black suits, nodding as if to acknowledge a colleague or two.

As he approached the dead old man's office he noticed something, it was small at first then one after another more appeared…flies, small black germ disease carrying flies, trying to get into the old man's office….or were they trying to get out?

Moving towards the door still keeping an eye out for anyone noticing him approaching he leant his back against it at the same time trying the handle. The low hum of the flies gathering in the air around him seemed to grow in it's intensity as he pushed the door, it opened into the office as a loud whoosh could be heard. A massive swarm of flies shot out like a bullet filling the entrance hall with the tiny black insects, every man scattered swiping at their heads to rid their eyes and ears of the invading insects. Jack took this diversion to shut himself in the room, his back right up against the door, eyes closed.

When he opened them he couldn't believe what greeted him, there was the odd fly still lingering but it was what was in the middle of the room that shocked him most. The wheelchair used by the old man stood right in the centre, and in it........was the old man himself, white almost grey in colour with a haunting grimace on his face, the last look of sheer terror as the last bit of stale smelling breath left his body or in his case was forced to stay in by the pressure of a pillow that should have brought comfort not death.

Jack slowly approached the body, it wasn't as if he was going to suddenly get up but with his track record of missions you just didn't know!

As he looked closely at the old man's agonising expression a single fly crept out of his mouth. Jack shot back but soon composed himself. His knee knocked the chair, as it did the old man's right hand fell, as it did something fell from his clutching claw like fingers......a golden Faberge egg!

It rolled along the dusty carpet and stopped short of the door, Jack ran after it picking it up, as he did so he must have accidently touched a switch as the whole thing opened up revealing a small golden teddy bear, he stared at the beauty of the intricacy of the work that must have gone into it. It took a few seconds for it to sink in, why would anyone kill the old man and leave the egg?

Still holding it he slowly turned to look at the old man just as a swarm of flies seeped out of his mouth releasing a cloud of stale air, for a split second he could have sworn the old man moved. Almost dropping the egg he stumbled back managing to keep a grip on it, just.

Suddenly his whole head was surrounded by the tiny black flies, he swotted some away to no avail, the door on which he was leaning pushed forward as if someone was trying to get in, he instinctively pushed back until he heard a small voice.

"Jack it's me Robbie let me in please before someone clocks me!!!"

Jack let go of the door and opened it quickly he grabbed his friend dragging him in shutting the door behind them, both sighing a breath of short lived relief as the flies seemed to have multiplied ten fold. The whole room was full of them, it was as if darkness had filled the room.

Robbie took his baseball hat off and started swiping at them frantically, spitting the odd dead one out of his mouth, the pair of them seemed to be dancing around the room trying to get away from the annoying little creatures.

The door swung open and two Russians stood silhouetted against the hallway, they shouted something in Russian then began spraying the air with what Jack and Robbie were hoping was fly spray!!

Slowly the air began to clear of flies but was now filled with a horrible smell, silence replaced the manic behaviour, the two of them momentarily relaxed and stood staring at the men who just stood staring back at them, no one moved.......the dead old man let out another stray bubble of air from his tar covered lungs which sounded like a groan making everyone turn to look at him.

Whilst the two Russians ran towards the old man Jack and Robbie made a run for the door pushing their way through the throng of men back towards the basement door. Angry voices shouting back at them then at another mass of flies that engulfed the whole of the entrance hallway again, turning it into a mass of men waving their arms about trying to swot as many flies as they possible could failing miserably, to the untrained eye they all looked like they were doing a traditional Russian dance.....badly!

Jack and Robbie ran through the basement door and started for the exit until one of the other rats beckoned for them to follow him towards the back of the building and outside amongst the rubble and ruins. They stumbled across the grounds literally, it was hard work but they soon reached the metal door of the 'shed' they had seen from the rooftop earlier.

One of the rats stood on top of another to key in a code number on the entrance pad, the sound of about ten computerised locks unlocking could be heard, Jack was getting impatient, they needed to get in ASAP in case they were being followed. Thankfully they didn't have to wait long when the door wooshed open, running in as the door closed quickly behind them.

Silence, the room was cold and had one metal door leading out of it, they tried pushing it, nothing happened until the rats repeated what they did outside using the same code.

Yet again the door wooshed open revealing a massive room with a table big enough to seat over a hundred men. It was a simple dark wooden table, nothing fancy, the chairs, red velvet high backed, each seating had a microphone so everyone could be heard in the vast high ceiling room.

On the dark walls hung portraits of past Russian Presidents, one portrait in particular stood out at the head of the room, a long haired man with dark piercing eyes, it was so life like you would think it was a two way screen and he was looking at you.

"Who the heck is that, he looks familiar.......he looks a bit like the man I saw leaving through the gate earlier?!!!" Robbie shuddered at the sight of the portrait which was bigger than all the others, it was definitely the same guy, you couldn't mistake those dark black piercing eyes.

Jack wasn't listening, he had his own ideas.

"That's, no it cant be but why would he be hung in here, he's been dead for years.......unless.....oh my lord this takes everything to another level, a very dangerous level!"

Robbie turned to look up at Jack confused as to what he was talking about.

"That man is the one man the Royal family trusted and worshipped .....Rasputin!"

Robbie almost fell over on the spot, Jack was almost deafened when he heard Tim exclaim in his ear piece "WHAT?!!!!!!!"

So there was someone on the inside after all who had a hand in the downfall of the Russian Royal family, the one person no one would have even thought of.

But how can he be involved, Rasputin was brutally murdered in 1916.

Jack and Robbie stood rooted to the spot staring at the huge black and white picture as the eyes bored into their souls, they both shivered.

"Jack I can sense movement, you need to get out of there, I think we have enough information for now, your safety is the main thing, MOVE! NOW!!."

Jack grabbed Robbie by the sleeve and dragged him towards the door, the other rat's followed close behind, as they opened the heavy metal door a few inches muffled voices could be heard entering the main entrance. Everyone turned on their heels and ran towards the back of the large room, towards the red velvet chairs then stopped. There was no sign of an exit, no door's, the walls were covered in the same pleated red velvet, there had to be some sort of exit surely.

Standing around trying to think of a plan of escape a small rat ran towards the picture of 'Rasputin', pulling back the red curtain that covered the wall under the picture he revealed a hidden door, padded in red leather and luckily unlocked.

He waited for the others to catch up with him so that someone tall enough could open it. The door opened onto a dark corridor that led to the left for about 100 yards then left again for quite a way. They all ran along the velvet ensconced corridor, thick pile carpet underfoot. Jack stopped suddenly, the others hadn't noticed at first when they did they looked at him as if to say 'why?'

"By my calculations guys this corridor is leading us back to the main building of the embassy. We need to find another way out and fast."

Tim scanned the grounds with his inbuilt radar system, eventually he found a secondary tunnel also to the left of the one they were in and luckily it led them right back to the area where the old wooden gate was situated. He relayed the information to them and it wasn't long until they found another hidden door to the tunnel and were running along towards the safer option of an exit.

When they reached the end they were horrified to find the door boarded up.

"Out of the way guy's.....aaaaaaaaaaaarrrrggghhhhhhh!!!!!"

Robbie went flying through the air in karate style kicking the wooden boards so hard they actually splintered into pieces, he landed bowed and turning he opened the door, allbe it just the remaining fragments of what used to be a door!! No one knew what to do for a split second then they all ran towards the daylight that was now streaming in, they found themselves behind the bin area, the wooden gate in the near distance....... freedom and safety.

Tim was waiting on the outside, everyone crammed in the back of him with some in the front passenger side, Jack obviously in the driving seat. Within seconds they were back in the busy tea time traffic on their way to the MI5 headquarters and some relative safety, but at the back of Jack's mind he wasn't too sure how safe they were now that he knew the Russians had the ability to listen in on the MI5 headquarters, something had gone radically wrong with the British security, the Chief was going to be furious.

# CHAPTER TWENTY TWO

The room filled up with men in black suits, slowly the red velvet chairs began to fill up with the agents of the Mother country.

Silence hung low in the room as the lights dimmed, some men moved uncomfortably in their seats, the atmosphere cooled, the air was thick with what could only be described as fear itself. These were the toughest men in Russia and still they feared one man, how could he have such a hold over so many?

Suddenly the room filled with a bright light almost blinding, music blared out of speakers in each corner as if announcing the arrival of royalty, back home in Russia it would probably have been.

Towards the back of the room where the huge black and white picture of Rasputin hung the door below opened slowly to reveal....... a tall long haired man with piercing eyes, eyes not unlike the ones staring from above the doorway, Rasputin's eyes, either side of him stood two large lions, heads held high as if sniffing the air for their prey, neither of them moved away from their master. No one dare move for fear of frightening the big cats.

Sat in a dark corner unseen by anyone.....so far, was a little rat, shaking in fear but excited at the same time. He had got separated from everyone else and being so small couldn't open the door on his own so had to hide until he could sneak out with one of the men.

He couldn't believe his eyes when Rasputin entered the room, surely the guy had been dead for years, all the rats knew the history of the Russian royal family and Rasputin. He seemed to have an air about him, it was as if he oozed power, instilling fear in everyone at the same time.

Who in their right mind would have lions as escorts in this day and age?

Joe (the rat) sensed that the lions could smell him hence them sniffing the air, he really hoped they couldn't smell the fear that suddenly swept over him.

He took the opportunity of everyone concentrating on Rasputin's entrance and the lions to run and sit under the massive table, it was so big no one would notice him under there plus if the lions lunged for him the men would be in the way and all hell would break loose.

He sat and tried to listen to what was happening, the music seemed to go on forever, dreary mind numbing music, he almost fell asleep. Perhaps that was the intention, put everyone into a trance and take over their minds.

The footwell of the table was soon filled with feet, all wearing the same shiny black shoes, all part of the 'uniform'. The music stopped. The man at the head of the table sat down, the hundreds of feet followed.

The man began to talk, his voice raspy with a heavy Russian accent, his words echoing around the vast room.

"It is time to fulfill my grandfather's wishes, to end the reign of the Romanovs once and for all. His first attempts obviously failed miserably, but this time we will make sure no one survives, I want revenge for his brutal murder, I want the blood of the Russian Royal family to be shed once more, this time onto the streets of this God forsaken city of greed, selfish debauched pit of constant sin. My mother tried but failed in her revenge but she started what I intend to finish hahahahaha" His deep laugh grew louder and louder like a mad man finally losing all sense of reality.

Joe sensed this man was angry and very bitter. He jumped suddenly as every man sat around the table banged their fists onto the tabletop in support, the noise was thunderous, almost deafening. He decided it was time to leave, he needed to get to Jack and Tim, this was an important development.

He heard music to his ears, the squeak of wheels and rattling of crockery, the tea trolley had arrived which meant he had transport out of here as soon as tea was served. He waited his turn and as the trolley was leaving he jumped aboard, hiding underneath the crisp white table cloth. The trip seemed to go on for a while but as soon as he sensed daylight as it exited the tunnel and was about to enter the kitchen at the back of the embassy he made his escape, a maid screamed as she saw him screaming in Russian 'vermin'....cheek thought Joe!

Running as fast as he could he made his way towards the same exit the lads used earlier, the old wooden gateway. Out of there and onto the streets of London, momentarily startled at the rush of busy teatime traffic he managed to calm himself enough to start running, running for his life. A bullet whizzed past his head as he started his fast paced marathon in search of his friends, more bullets flew through the air as he darted in and out of the traffic, horns blowing, women screaming at the sight of a rat in daylight!

Joe stopped to rest a minute, for a young rat he was really out of shape, his breathing heavy he leant against a lampost, fear ripped into his body as fast cars whizzed past the city noise was deafening almost so overpowering he might lose all sense of where to go next.

"Joe, Joe where yer wanna go mate?" A London black taxi like Tim loomed over him waiting for an answer.

"MI5 headquarters, I need to get there ASAP." Relief washed over him, it certainly paid to have friends in high places in this city.

"Hop in, I'll have yer there in no time." Joe jumped in, seat belt on, and as the taxi shot off into the traffic he realised why it had been a good idea to strap himself in, the G force threw him back in his seat pinning him down, he actually sank into the leather of the seat almost being swallowed up by it!!

# CHAPTER TWENTY THREE

Tim parked back in the underground garage in the MI5 headquarters, rat after rat piled out onto the cold cement floor. Boris walked round to where Jack was standing, he heard him talking to Tim.

"Well that was interesting, mind you it's hardly surprising that the Russians would have an underground meeting room. The portrait is obviously a descendant of Rasputin but which one?"

"He is an evil man, a very evil man Sir." Boris's eyes were wide with fear.

"Why the hell would his portrait be hanging in the meeting room of the Russians unless....I need to talk to the Chief." With that Jack was off running up the stairs to the Chief's office, forgetting his small Russian friends.

Running through the dimly lit corridors the only sound was the thumping of his feet on the carpet. The walls were so thick you could not hear anything from the outside world, it was as if the city was literally another world away.

Banging on the Chief's door he didn't wait for an invitation to go in. The Chief looked startled at the sudden noisy intrusion but realising it was Jack he rolled his eyes as if to say 'here we go!'

"Sir I think I know who was behind the death of the Romanovs, they had someone on the inside that was not an ally but acted as one."

The Chief frowned at him to get to the point, sitting back in his chair he waited for Jack to do the big reveal, little did he know how it would impact on the situation.

"Rasputin sir, he was working for the Russians NOT the family, he was the man on the inside." Jack dropped into the seat opposite the Chief who in turn looked like he'd seen a ghost.

"Why in God's name would he be involved in their demise, he led everyone to believe he had an strange interest in the girls and their mother?" He couldn't get his head around this latest bit of news.

"I have no idea Sir but the room we found in the underground bunker was massive and the table could fit at least 100 people round it, it all seemed very well organised and well er like a NATO headquarters, the only thing missing was a large red button for some psycho to press." Jack thought to himself that if they had had more time he was sure they would have found such a button. Rasputin was well known for being mad, you just had to look at his eyes in the portrait to believe it and the stories that he had spent many hours with girls and their mother, rumour had it that there was a very unhealthy relationship going on there with all of them. Just thinking about it made his skin crawl.

It wasn't long before Joe turned up at the garage door, the taxi managed to get a message through to Tim to let him in. Without waiting for the door to rise fully he ran underneath it racing up to Tim excited to tell him the latest information, once he had spoken to him he was sent up to the Chief's office where he found the hallway full of his rat friends who had followed Jack up. There were so many there he had to push his way through to the office door where he banged as hard as he could. Jack let him in, standing back so he could rush up to the Chief.

"Rasputin had a hand in the deaths of the Romanovs."

"We know!!" Everyone shouted as one!!

Joe gawped to one then the other 'how?'

"He's still alive!!!" One of the rats shouted.

"How can he be, he would be ancient......hang on." The Chief typed something on his keyboard....tap tap tap tap....

"He had children, Maria, Varvara, Anna...and two sons, Dmitri and Georgiy. One of the boys must be taking on his mantle, taken over from where his mad father left off. His body disappeared, who's to say he was actually dead anyway. If Anastasia can survive then I'm sure as hell that Rasputin could. We need to find someone else on the inside that knows more information."

"Or it could be a grandson." Tim butted in from down in the depths of the garage.

Jack looked at the Chief they both nodded in agreement with Tim, it was another possibility for them to ponder, and the age of the man they saw indicated that was more likely.

The room filled up with rat's, everyone stood around waiting for someone to speak, looking at each other, no one said a word, until Boris came bounding in.

"His grandson Dimitri, he is zee one who idolised his grandfather and took on as you say his grandfather's mantle. I did not realise zis until today when I saw the portrait, all ze pieces of the puzzle fell into place, those dark evil eyes are the same that Dimitri has, no mistake. He killed Yurovsky and possibly Maxim, the old man was incapable of being any threat but Dimitri ated him and Maxim had outlived his use.

Yurovsky Snr wanted Rasputin dead and was behind the so called assassination of the man, he was furious when he realised that Rasputin had somehow survived even more so when no one could find any trace of him.

Rasputin's daughter Maria had a hand in his escape and took her father to Paris where he eventually died of his injuries. It was a long and painful death and Maria grew more and more bitter as he lingered in agony, promising revenge on Yurovsky and Anastasia. Yes she knew the young girl had survived, Maria was psychic like her father and foretold the young girl's survival and how she would escape. That is why she left with her father to Paris. It took years after her father's death to locate Anastasia, miraculously they had been socialising in the same circles all along but Maria never recognised her, even her psychic powers failed her this time."

Jack and the Chief stood open mouthed staring at Boris, so did every rat in the room, how in God's name did he know all of this? As he realised everyone was looking at him he carried on talking......

"My father was a pet of the young Alexei, the young boy loved him so much that when Anastasia was rescued she took him with her...... his cage had been trashed and he ran out into the grounds, he found her alf buried and licked her face to bring her round from that day forth she took him with her on that long journey to freedom in memory of her brother."

The Chief dropped into his chair as did Jack into his totally gobsmacked at what they were hearing!!

"Lions, the man has lions, two of them to be precise, can you explain that one?" Joe butted in trying not to be left out with his information.

Everyone looked at Boris for his input but the Chief had this one.....

"Maria, Rasputin's daughter left Paris the night before Anastasia's husbands murder in the park, she had ordered the Russians to kill him but had to be out of the country so as to not be accused of being involved. However the one small detail that gave her involvement away was the lion claw marks on Louis's face, Maria had two pet lions which were left behind, and her men used them in the murder of Louis. She had travelled to the States but when the police realised her part in the man's death they froze all her assets of which there was great wealth. She needed to earn a living and having had experience with her lion's she joined a circus, always on the move, never in one city or the same circus long enough to leave a solid trail for the police to find and follow. She eventually became a lion tamer and fell in love with a fellow circus performer, they had a son….."

"The man in the portrait!!!" Everyone including Jack and the Chief shouted in unison.

"Yes exactly, the portrait isn't Rasputin but his grandson, he has come to revenge the death of his grandfather and mother who was brutally murdered also but by who and why we have no idea….yet"

Jack and the chief sat dumb struck, the floor was covered in silent rodents. Boris stood in the middle of them all looking from one to another waiting for someone to speak.

# CHAPTER TWENTY FOUR

Back at the embassy Dmitri paced the dining room where he had had Maxim shot, there was no trace of his murder, the Russians were experts on cover ups.

He knew that Darya was now well ensconced in the headquarters of MI5 and probably telling all that she knew which luckily for him was not a lot but sadly for her it was enough to sign a death warrant on her. Then there was the added problem of the best agent MI5 had ever had, Jack Courage. He had spotted him a couple of times earlier at the embassy, Dmitri was always on the prowl, silently keeping an eye on his 'domain' and the hoard of men under his charge, Jack Courage had assumed no one had seen him but Dmitri had, he always 'saw' everything that was going on.

No one would suspect him of murder, why would he dirty his own hands when he had so many men at his beck and call. It was all so easy, he could come and go as he pleased which he did again tonight. He made his way to the headquarters of MI5 and stood opposite the building in the shadows staring up at the windows wondering which room Darya would be in.

It wasn't long until he caught a glimpse of her staring out onto the dimly lit street below, he edged forward into the yellow glow of the street lamp in the hope that she might see him, he laughed quietly to himself as he saw her hand shoot to her throat in fear as their eyes locked, he pointed his cocked fingers at her in a shooting position, she knew her days were numbered as he pretended to fire an executional bullet at her. Laughing loudly he walked away, but this time he forgot to hide his face as the outside security cameras caught him perfectly or was that his intention?

Darya lent against the cold glass, small droplets of rain slid down as did the terrified tears on her young cheeks.

Jack came up behind her and placed a friendly hand on her shoulder startling her momentarily.....

"You're safe here, he can't get to you. We've got our surveillance team following him as we speak. He's only trying to scare you"

"It is working." Her clipped Russian accent quivered as she looked at Jack. She turned and walked away from the window, from the threat that lingered on the other side of the glass which may be bulletproof but nothing is ever Dmitri proof, he will find a way to get to her if not tonight another time.

# CHAPTER TWENTY FIVE

Antonio sat in his armchair, he'd fallen asleep. Alex crept quietly over to him crouching to pick up something that had fallen from his aged hand to the floor. It was an old photograph of a beautiful young girl holding a teddy bear with her, a young boy and three other girls. It had been ripped up in the past and now held together with sellotape. Alex studied it closely, he gasped at the sight of the bear in her arms, the very same bear his father had obtained at the auction only this one didn't have the special belly button but it was definitely the same bear. He knew his history, he knew straight away who the people in the picture were, and now why the Russians were following his father, the pieces of the puzzle had finally started to fit together, seeing that his father was still asleep he took it on himself to put an end to this nightmare.

He glanced around as he raised his collar against the light rain that fell as he made his way out onto the streets of the capital city hailing a taxi.

"Where to guvnor?"

"The Russian Embassy please." Alex was getting himself comfy as a voice filled the cab.

"Why the Embassy Alex, what would your father say?" Tim automatically locked all doors and implemented the bulletproof protection that completely encased him. The Russians would have Alex's movements covered at all times.

Alex shot round at the vocal intrusion, confused as to who had spoken, he stopped dead as he realised there was no one in the driving seat. His knuckles went white with fear as they gripped the edge of his seat.

"Who the hell are you? I need to go to the embassy and tell them to leave us alone, my father is old and weak and can't take much more of this living in constant fear."

"And you think running to them and pleading with them that they will just roll over and do as you ask, I don't think so do you? So why are you really going to the embassy?" Tim's voice was dark, he knew there was more to this visit than Alex was letting on.

"You won't get out of my cab until you tell me the truth, and believe me I will know if you are lying."

Alex panicked looked around for a way out, trapped he couldn't think fast enough, he wasn't cut out for all this spying lark, he knew he had to quit while he was ahead if only for his father's sake.

"I want my father safe, the bear isn't really worth anything financially although my father paid so much for it. It's all politics at the end of the day and if whatever comes out is detrimental to the Russian government then that's their problem not my father's."

"Alex, you really have no idea do you what this will mean for Russia or even your own adoptive country? There has been a massive cover up on the murders of the Russian Royal family and the survival of it's Royal line, plus the fact the Russian government knew all of this and have made it their mission over the years to silence all involved, many people have died horrendous deaths along the way, needless deaths that the government would have to pay for if found to be involved. Politically it will bring down the government, no government is beyond the law to the extent they can cover this up."

"Oh dear lord." Alex groaned, frustration and fear all mixed in with confusion.

"I'll take you home." Tim turned to drive Alex back to his father's house, that's when he noticed Dmitri lurking in the shadows smiling knowingly. It would only be a matter of time until someone caved and gave in to the one that held all the cards, he laughed at Alex as Tim drove past not realising the taxi was filming him as he did so, any evidence no matter how small was another nail in the Russian Governments proverbial coffin.

Tim called through to MI5 and arranged for someone to visit Antonio and assign protection for him and Alex. They were to stay in their own home so as to not bring any attention to the fact it was known that they knew the Russians were involved but Tim couldn't take any chances and had to make sure the two men were kept alive. Once protection arrived he left to put an end to this nightmare once and for all.

# CHAPTER TWENTY SIX

It was gone midnight when Jack arrived at Kensington Palace, Ana was waiting for him in her plush sitting room with Alexandria and her loyal maid, Sofina.

Sofina was the Granddaughter of Sofia Ivanovna Tyutcheva one of the governess's that looked after the girls when they were young. She and her Grandmother Sofia had managed to leave Russia before the family tragedy when Sofia was sacked for going against Rasputin. They had made their way to Paris to be with other Romanov family members who had also managed to leave Russia before the tragedy. They stayed with Grand Duchess Xenia Alexandrovna of Russia. Eventually Sofina was reunited with Anastasia in Paris after her escape where she made it her job to look after her again with Ana and Alexandria and go wherever they went.

The room was lit only by candles, it was soothing and kept the women calm, it was as if they were back home in Paris.

"I have information proving who was and is behind what happened to you and your family. I think you all need to sit down, this is going to be hard enough for me to tell you let alone for you to understand." Jack wasn't sure how to tell them what had been going on all of these years or how they would take it, but one thing he knew, he had to tell them everything, full disclosure.

"It appears that the Russian Government had found someone who could infiltrate your family unit and get all the information on you they needed, but the one person they used also incriminated you against your own country on behalf of the

Bolshevik Secret Police. Whatever you did the infiltrator made sure you were seen in a bad light, your country slowly believed the lies and began to detest you all for all the wrong reasons."

Ana stood at the window with her back to him as he spoke, gazing out onto the park, shadows danced as the overhead clouds glided along the moonlit sky. Was that a shadow or another Russian in the undergrowth? She wasn't sure but at this point she really didn't care, she felt like she had gone back in time and her life was crumbling around her all over again. How many people had she trusted over the years, how many had let her down? She had only ever trusted her husband, her daughter, Sam Duggan, Sofina and Verene, oh how she hoped now that none of them were to be mentioned as the ones that had double crossed her.

"Ana, the one person who brought all of this on you was........ Rasputin." The silence was deafening, apart from the gasps from the maid and Alexandria.

Ana was emotionless as always. But Jack noticed her back stiffen, slowly she turned to face him.

"If you think I am shocked your wrong Jack, my mother was always afraid of him. He filled everyone with fear, my grandmother however seemed to be in awe of him for some reason. She always defended him no matter what, even when my mother and aunts pleaded with her to stop him coming into their rooms. Nowadays you would call it grooming, he called it cleansing of evil spirits, saying the country thought they were possessed and he was their saviour. Of course my grandmother was totally taken in by him and believed everything he told her. She was an unwitting conspirator of her own family's demise, she would lock herself away in her room for hours faining ill health, turning a blind eye to the terror he cleverly brought down on our family."

"My aunts adored my mother and always protected her, protected her to the very end. When that fateful night came in the cellar as the bullets began to rain down on them they flung themselves onto her in protection, but the one thing that protected her more than their bodies was the love of Alexander the young soldier who loved her."

"But he wasn't there Ana." Jack interrupted her and instantly regretted it.

"He didn't have to be there, the Bear he gave her saved her life, the belly button is the one bullet that was meant for her heart Jack."

"Oh my lord, the one bit of evidence against the Secret Police that could bring them down, they used their own special bullets for the execution only a certain amount were made to be used."

"Yes but there is one left, all the others were......" She struggled with the words..... "Drunkenly dug out of the bodies, somehow thankfully they missed my mother else they would have realised she was still alive. Thinking all cases were retrieved they thought no evidence was left behind."

"Only one bullet was missed......!" Jack whispered his words in shock.

"Yes, the one in the bear. It was years until they found out about this one piece of evidence, they had only hunted my mother because of the fact people had assumed she had survived and they wanted to finish the job, thinking no one would know either way but when the story of the bear came about they began to panic. Then another servant Anna Demedova who had somehow followed my mother to Paris overheard my mother talking about it one night and greed took hold. She stole the bear alerting the Russians at the same time. She sold her to the Old Regime, she signed my mother's death warrant."

Jack dropped to a nearby chair at what she had relayed to him, so much sadness, so much pain, the unconditional love of the sisters protecting their Anastasia and the love of a young soldier that subsequently unwittingly saved her life.

Why would a government chase a young woman through her life, for what gain? Why not let her live, what harm could she do?

"My grandfather knew who in the government was stealing from our country, not only valuables but also political secrets that could have started a world war where there would have been no winners, just casualties, many many casualties. My grandfather wanted to stop the blood shed, the Regime wanted to go to war with the rest of the world. The fact that my mother may or may not be out there free stopped the war, they couldn't take the chance that if they implemented any attacks that she would come forward with any evidence against them. My grandfather had kept records of everything he knew, even I don't know what happened to them but someone does but I have no idea who."

"But the Russians still think you do and that is why they continue to hunt you down."

"Yes." Ana finally relaxed and sat down, slightly deflated but at the same time as if a great weight had been lifted off of her royal shoulders.

"The bullet is the beginning of the fall of the old and new Regime, the evidence my grandfather accumulated over the years is the final nail in the country's coffin. The only real coffins though were the cheap ones my ancestors were buried in." Finally a tear fell. Alexandria reached out and took hold of her mother's hand to comfort her, Ana nodded.

"So who has the evidence and where?" Jack was really stumped this time.

Tim's system was working over time and still he came up with zilch, not a single clue. The Romanov family tree automatically came to his attention, as they say everything happens for a reason and Tim thought there must be a reason why the tree came up. He had studied it before but this time something or rather someone stood out to him, someone who was close to Tsar Nicholas but according to the history books he had let the Romanovs down at the last minute.

Surely the one person standing out wouldn't have got involved in keeping Russian Governmental Secrets, how could he?

Tim delved deeper into all the information he had on both men trying to find a time or times when the two met up, cross matching events with the secret police, missing persons, political disturbances and British Royal Visits to Russia.

It seems that one person who had political and Royal protection may be involved in smuggling Tsar Nicholas's stolen documents that could have easily brought the whole of Russia down. The one thing that confused Tim was....why were the papers never revealed?

He radioed through to Jack who didn't answer straight away, Tim knew the conversation would be a long and traumatic one but this new piece of information was crucial to finding a way to end this endless nightmare and possibly keeping Ana and Alexandria safe for the rest of their lives.

"Jack I'm sorry to interrupt you but I think I may have found some very interesting information which I REALLY NEED YOU TO LOOK AT."

By the way Tim was talking with such urgency Jack realised the importance of what he may have to say and made his excuses to leave the ladies for a few minutes.

He made his way down to where his partner was parked, he looked towards the park, in the distance the city lights that offered hope and fear, but closer, the eerie shadows of the tree filled grounds surrounded the palace. For a split second he felt chilled to his bones, was he being watched by the Russians? A shadow moved in the distance, a bird's shrill scream cried out.

Walking over to Tim he wrapped his arms around himself against the cold and the psychological chill that engulfed him.

"Ok what's the latest?" Jack sat in the driver's seat and waited for his partner to fill him in on what he had discovered.

His heart jumped when the name rang through the speaker system, surely Tim had got in wrong, everyone knew the man in question was hard and tough, and didn't always go along with Royal protocol but over the years that was classed as part of his character that people admired him for but this was way out there. Worse than when the country accused Edward VIII of being a Nazi sympathiser.

"Are you sure he inherited the files"

"Who would think that a member of the British Royal Family would be smuggling documents out of Russia? Just the mere accusation could start a war and that was the last thing the Russians wanted at the time as it would get in the way of their plans to eradicate their own royal family without bringing more attention to themselves. When he died he left the files in his will to the one person who could be trusted to keep them safe until they needed to be used should that need ever arise, and was closely related to the Tsar."

"So Ana and Alexandria are not only being protected by our Royal family because of their family connections but also because one of our very own royals is involved to such an extent it could endanger him. Do you think the girls know he's involved?"

"I don't think so Jack by the way Ana was talking, I've only just found the information out myself."

"I think you're right? We haven't much time, with Dmitri Rasputin's blatant involvement he must think he has us running scared. We are running but not away from him." Jack got out of Tim without saying another word and made his way back into the palace to talk to Ana, he was convinced she knew more than she was letting on. He knew she had kept many many secrets over the years to protect herself, mother and daughter but it was time to start trusting the right people and divulging everything she knew, everything she had spent years trying to forget to save her own sanity and life.

As Jack entered the room he realised something was different, the three women had hats and coats on with hand luggage beside them.

It was time to move on again, but this time Jack wasn't letting them go.....not without him or Tim that is.

"Right we are going straight to MI5 headquarters where no one and I mean no one will be able to get to you. And when we are there you can tell me who your contact here is."

Ana looked right into his eyes, poker face.

"Who is he Ana?" Jack wasn't leaving until she admitted what she knew.

"I have no idea what or who you are talking about Mr Courage." This time she flinched fractionally, Jack was trained, he knew body language, she was hiding something, hiding someone.

"Ok let me tell you who your contact is........" He waited for her to jump in to either stop him or tell him what he wanted to know......her knuckles went white, her tension was rising, still she didn't say a word. Her mouth opened then closed.

"Your father's contact was none other than a family member, someone who only had a limited contact with him on very few occasions. When your father needed to get more files to him he used embassy servants so as to not bring any suspicions on important staff members, if any of them were to be found to be involved then the political fallout would almost cause a war of its own, but using servants was easier as they were never privy to any important information and couldn't get their hands on it so they would never be under suspicion. Your father was very clever and found out in time who he could trust and used them to smuggle files out of the embassy, even handing them to his contact for him. Some even travelled to England to deliver them personally but they never came back as it was too dangerous but the contact made sure they were rehoused with different identities for their own safety, and he left them in his will when he died they were handed down to another high profile person. But the British government was involved the whole time, it was a small secretive group housed inside a certain building............Buckingham Palace. It was well known in the history books that George V and your grandfather were close and both had the same political views. King George had great plans to get your ancestors out of the country alive and to safety in his country, our country but someone in the secret police got wind of this and brought the plan of your family's demise closer.

Our King sadly couldn't get anyone to Russia quick enough to get your family out alive in time. His men literally arrived at the Ipatiev house hours too late, however thanks to a young boy who had found Anastasia half buried alive he was able to smuggle her out of the country with the help of his family. Whilst some of the country mourned the Romanovs, George mourned his cousin's death, guilt at not getting to him and his family in time. He took all this guilt and information to his grave but it was all recorded with the files he and Nicholas had accumulated over the years to be used at a later date. Everything was handed down to one man no one would suspect..........Prince Philip the Queens husband, Anastasia's mother was his Grand Aunt, he was 15 when King George died and left him the files. It was a great responsibility at such a young age but it was almost as if it was a duty he had no choice but to take on......" Jack looked at Ana's ashen shocked face, he knew then that he and Tim were right.

"Jack it's time we left for headquarters.... please we don't have much time."

Jack couldn't understand why Tim was in such a hurry but managed to get the three women to gather their luggage, allowing them to pack more as they were going to nearby safety and not on the run as they first had thought.

With the women safely in the back Jack put the privacy glass up so that he could talk to Tim in private.

"Ok, what was the rush to get us out?" Jack drove Tim away from the palace and turned left eventually making his way into the night traffic, at such a late hour there was very little around.

"The grounds were swarming with Russians Jack, the place must be bugged."

"Oh hell that means Prince Philip is in danger as well, I'll call through to the Chief."

"Already done."

"Of course it is."

Jack knew he could rely on Tim to be on the ball and not waste any time in protecting the Prince.

Alexandria gasped as she looked out of the back of the window, she had seen at least ten men in black just stood staring at Tim as he drove them away.

Ana grabbed her hand squeezing it tightly, the end of the nightmare was in sight, the only thing they didn't know was how it was going to end. With her head held high Ana knew they had to be brave, many secrets were going to come out to the public soon, a war may ensue but for once they could feel some sort of relief that they don't have to hide anymore or......run.

# CHAPTER TWENTY SEVEN

Tim gained speed, Jack had no control over the steering wheel as usual. Gradually he drove faster and faster, no one really noticed until he screeched round a corner.

"Tim what the hell is going on?" Jack swung round in his seat to try and look out of the back window, experience told him they were probably being followed, sure enough there was a black limo behind them with blacked out windows so no chance of seeing who was in there but he knew it was the Russians..... the red flag on the bonnet gave it away!! They're not even hiding the fact that they are following them anymore!

The women looked at the car then Jack, eyes pleading for help.

"Don't worry ladies, we've got this under control....ouch!" Jack fell against the side of the cab as Tim swerved round another corner at speed, the driver behind put his foot down to try and keep up. The women slipped all over the seat trying not to fall off as Tim swerved from side to side. In the distance they caught sight of the large MI5 headquarters, they could just make out the garage doors slowly rising, just as they thought they were home and dry another black Russian car appeared from nowhere stopping in front of the garage doors that carried on opening, this time the drivers window was open and as Tim got closer Jack caught sight of the tall Russian from the auction, the look on his face as Tim gained on him at speed was priceless, he could see the fat Russian panicking and from his hand movements Jack would say he was trying to persuade the tall one to move out of the way ASAP. He put his foot down seconds before impact, Tim caught the back bumper as he hit him, spinning the Russian embassy car 360 degrees, the women screamed, the two Russians screamed.

Tim drove straight onto the ramp and drove into the underground garage as the doors shot down quicker than they went up.

Silence…….no one dared speak….no one had the ability to do so for a few minutes.

"WOW" was all Ana could say, Alexandria and Sofina looked at her in shock at the unlady-like reaction from the woman!

"I think it's best we get up stairs and talk to the Chief. You're safe now ladies, no one and I mean no one can get to you now."

Jack got out of Tim and helped them out, the three of them looked around as if to make sure they were actually safe. There was no way anyone, not even the Russians could get to them here, the striking elegance of the women brought an old fashioned beauty to the cold concrete surroundings.

Ana looked at him, as the other two were taken up stairs, for what seemed like minutes she stared at Jack trying to find the right words, a simple thank you didn't seem enough. But that's all she could find at the moment.

"Thank you Jack, thank you." For the first time he saw her smile, he saw a difference in her eyes, he saw life, as if the years of fear had been washed away, as if her life was beginning all over again…….perhaps the fairytale could have a happy ending after all.

The three women walked slowly along the dark corridors, this time not in an impending death but towards the beginning of a freedom they thought they would never feel.

As they reached the Chief's office the door slowly opened to reveal an old woman…..Anna Demidova, the maid that Anastasia believed double crossed her when she stole the Golden Teddy Bear.

Alexandria gasped as she recognised the traitor, Anna slowly moved towards her with arms outstretched to greet her stopping as she saw the look of horror on Ana's face.

"Oh Alexandria if only you and your mother knew the truth, please let me explain I beg just a few minutes of your time." Her old eye's filled with tears of regret.

"Ladies, allow me to do the explaining, please sit." Chief Gibson motioned to some chairs, he raised his eyebrows as if to say I'll explain that later as well when they noticed the amount of rats stood around on the floor!! Looking at the women in awe the rats curtsied.

The Chief stood with his back to the window as he began to explain Ms Demidova's part in the theft of the bear.

"Anna Demidova - survived the execution by curling up behind the Empresses chair. The soldiers left the bodies for hours, they lay in the basement while the men partied outside in the grounds. Then when drunk they decided to move the bodies. However whilst they were partying Anna managed to make her way out of the building and hide in the undergrowth only leaving when the men were busy burying the bodies in the shallow grave. She knew Anastasia had family in Paris and knowing her own life would be in danger if she was found she made her way there.

After a while she found the family and was hired as a maid out of sympathy and thanks for telling them what happened to your family in their last hours.

Eventually Anastasia arrived and a shocked Anna helped with Anastasia's new identity and was loyal for a while until one night when by chance she saw a Russian who recognised her from their home country, their eyes meet, fear fills Anna, her cover is blown she panics, if she has been recognised then she will compromise Anastasia's safety so she didn't double cross her after all, she left Paris to stop the Russians getting to her but she took the bear hoping to sell it and to take the heat off of where Anastasia was.

She moved to London, married a young man servant but the two of them had to keep on the move as the Russians would not leave them alone knowing she would have information on the execution as the 'only' survivor and if Anastasia had survived she would be the one to know and where she was now. Anna had a very large price on her head.

After years on the move around the world working for the gentry, hired through Anastasia's family contacts it all became too much and she needed to stop running, she needed to rest.

She put the bear up for sale under the instruction's of Prince Philip to draw the Russian's out into the open. MI5 had brought it to his attention that Dmitri was living in the Russian Embassy and had every intention of wreaking revenge on the death of his grandfather and mother, opening a whole can of worms which would blow your cover endangering your lives and possibly finally starting a cold war that his grandfather Rasputin and the Secret police had tried and failed to do all those years ago.

Anna Demedova saved Anastasia's life and her descendants all those years ago Alexandria and has made it her life's work to carry on doing so."

The Chief stopped talking, the room was silent, no one dared move let alone breath, the rats exchanged shocked looks.

Ana sat her old hands clasping her small bag, rising slowly she moved towards the old woman who she had spent so many years hating as did her mother. Holding her hand up as Anna tried to stand she knelt down in front of her and placed her hands on the old woman's lap then her head....just as she used to as a small child. Both women cried, tears of regret for not knowing the truth, for missing out on so many years of friendship. The old woman placed her hand on Ana's head slowly stroking her hair....

"Don't cry Malenkaya (little one) don't cry for what might have been, you lived to make your mother proud, to make your country proud."

Sofia and Ana cried quietly, every single rat sobbed holding onto each other for support, there wasn't a dry eye in the office. Even the Chief turned towards the window and wiped a tear away.

History was being made but it wasn't going to be that simple, there was still the matter of Rasputin's grandson who was on a path of bloody revenge which would result in the whole world getting involved, world war three would be implemented.....all because a young innocent woman survived a brutal execution.

Jack took this tender moment to take leave and when out in the corridor he ran as fast as he could back to Tim, who had heard everything.

He stood looking at his friend, silence.

He stood waiting for his side of the story, silence.

Without a single word being spoken by man or machine Jack got into the driving seat, started the engine himself and drove his friend towards the garage doors nodding acknowledgement to the man who opened them for him.

It was a while until the silence was broken.

"Tim how much more do you know, our country is at stake, the whole world is on the verge of going to war?" Jack's voice was calm but underlying anger simmered.

"Dmitri will stop at nothing to start a revolution against the rest of the world, he is mad enough to think that he and his men can take on the task. No one knows how many followers he has, the Russian Secret Police from the old revolutionary day's still practice now and have continued recruiting over the years but no one knows the identities of any of the members making it near impossible to fight. I'm sorry Jack I should have let you in sooner but it still wouldn't have made a difference where he is concerned, only for Sam."

Silence fell again as they both remembered the one man that literally laid down his life for a woman from another country, another life, he paid the ultimate price for such loyalty.

Jack realised they were outside the Russian Embassy.

"WOW someone's up late!"

Every single room was lit, people could be seen moving about in them, something was kicking off. Tim's radio crackled into life.

"Tim, Jack it's Gibson, Robbie and Boris are on their way to the Russian Embassy they have it on good authority that Dmitri is about to try and take control."

"Already there Sir, already there."

# CHAPTER TWENTY EIGHT

"What do you mean they are at the headquarters. You were supposed to stop them before they left the grounds." Dmitri was furious with his men, he never lost his temper, his calmness was more frightening, his dark eyes would pierce your very soul.

He walked slowly and purposefully over to the tall Russian and before he could do anything Dmitri grabbed the man by the throat with such force and speed he had his body against the wall with a thud. The short fat man stepped back almost falling over, he turned mid stumble aiming for the door. How Dmitri got to his side was impossible but he did and he still had the tall Russian in his grip, he'd dragged him across the room with him. He threw the tall Russian's body against the door still holding onto him, stopping the small man from leaving, his colleague slumped to the floor gasping for air, grabbing at Dmitri's hands trying to free his airway, within seconds he stopped struggling. Dmitri let the man fall to the floor, dead, the other man took a few steps back then closed his eyes waiting for the end to come, with one shot it was all over as Dmitri fired.

Dmitri walked the length of the large table, his hand caressing every chair as he did so, his domain, his office of power.

As he lifted his head towards the ceiling he roared like a lion then began to laugh like the mad man he was.

It was time to start the war on the very people who killed his grandfather and mother, somehow he would still find the woman who had caused them so much pain and trouble.....Anastasia, dead or alive, although he knew she would be dead by now he would make her descendants pay the price.

He turned towards the back of the room grinning at his own portrait, the door below opened as a tall man in black appeared with two leads, one in each hand on the other end was a white tiger, his mother's beloved babies.

The Russian walked slowly as did the lion's, they stopped in front of their master who knelt down to caress their fur.

"Leave us, go to the house and make the appropriate plans we will be leaving at sunrise." He stood with his hands on his lions heads, he could smell the Romanov blood already.

"Hahahahahaha" he laughed as the lions regally raised their heads and roared.

# CHAPTER TWENTY NINE

Dmitri walked to the large chair at the head of the huge table and sat down, he knew this would be the last time he would sit here. For a fleeting moment his own death flashed through his mind, he grunted in anger at himself for letting it even enter his mind.

Slamming his fist down on the table in frustration he began to go through why and how he had come to be sat there.

His grandfather Rasputin was hired by the Russian Bolshevik Secret police to infiltrate the Romanov family any way he could and spy on them, the secret police soon realised tho that he was actually a liability because of his strange and unhealthy behaviour towards the girls and decided he had to be dealt with and quickly.

He was ambushed late one night by a group of secret police where he was brutally beaten and stabbed, they left him to die half in half out of the Neva river not realising his daughter had witnessed the attack. She managed to get her brothers to help their father out of the freezing water and into hiding. He died weeks later, it was a long and painful death instilling so much bitterness in Maria his daughter that she made it her mission to find the missing Anastasia herself, after her father had predicted on his deathbed that she had actually managed to escape, Maria had the same psychic power as her father and travelled to Europe then onto Paris to find Anastasia.

She moved into a large house with her brothers, and two lions, she was classed as eccentric but never used her family name for fear of her life.

She grew suspicious of a woman who was going by the name Madam Bonaparte, her powers led her to believe she would somehow lead her to Anastasia. For years she kept a tail on the woman and her husband Louis, until the day one of their maids disappeared with the bear.

The poor woman thought she was helping her mistress but in fact her leaving suddenly in the middle of the night with the bear only proved to Maria that Madam Bonaparte was the one woman she had been hunting……Anastasia Romanov.

She ordered her brothers to kidnap Sam Duggan one night when he was meeting Anastasia's husband in the park, the two men fought back when the Russians attacked, sadly Louis didn't survive as one of Maria's pet lions managed to get loose from one of her brothers and attacked him with his claws, but as the Russian went to shoot the lion because it was out of control he shot Louis by mistake, either way Louis would have died. They left the body in the park with the lion's scratch mark on his face as they didn't have time to dispose of it. Taking Sam away as a hostage hoping to find out more regarding Anastasia……no matter what they did to him he never divulged any information on her situation or whereabouts.

Maria had already left Paris for America so that she couldn't be implicated in Louis's death. She joined a circus as a dancer in Chicago and travelled the country for years, she fell in love with a lion tamer with whom she had a son, Dmitri.

But back home in Russia Yakov Yurovsky had realised over the years she was on the same mission as him to find Anastasia he also realised she was more of a liability and had her brutally murdered, hence Vadim's death a few days ago.

Dmitri had only recently heard Vadim talking on the telephone to Maxim late one night that it was in fact his father who had had Maria eliminated and why. Vadim had unwittingly sealed Maxim's fate with that call, no witnesses were to be found.....alive.

The night that Maria died nothing seemed out of the ordinary to her. She had gone to the lion cages to see her 'babies'. On entering everything seemed normal but it was only when the cage door slammed behind her did she realise that the lions in front of her were not hers but two that resembled them, the noise of the gate shutting startled the animals. Maria looked from the now locked gate to the lions with a sudden rush of panic and fear, it was all over so quickly as they ripped her apart, nothing was left except the ring her father had given her which had been gifted him by the empress that formed part of the Romanov treasure collection.

Dmitri vowed revenge - if it wasn't for the Romanov family his mother and grandfather would have survived - plus he hated the Russian government for turning their backs on his family, he left America immediately after his mother's murder.

Dmitri looked at the same ring on his little finger with anger.

He had managed to get a job inside the Russian government, it was the only way he could plot his revenge and worked his way up, finally getting a posting to London, where he knew the trail of the bear and Anastasia had gone cold. But he knew she couldn't be too far away. Unbeknown to him the real reason his career in the Russian government was so easy was because of his family connections and reputation, the government wanted to keep an eye on him. Sending him to London kept him out of the Mother country and in the dark from important information......or so they thought.

For years he built up his own army of followers, building his own headquarters at the back of the main building, only the chosen few or in his case 'many' were allowed to enter.

It was either join his army or die, so no one really had a choice, and he always picked the best.

When the bear came up for sale he knew the end of his mission was close, he knew his revenge would soon be implemented, Romanov blood would be shed again.

The old man that bought the bear was just a minor nuscience, but when he realised who he was, the son of Anastasia's first and only love he let him live thinking he would lead him to the rest of the surviving Romanovs, if any.

The one person he didn't bank on was Jack Courage and his unusual side kick, a London Black taxi. Over the years he had seen Verene in the taxi but had no idea of the special abilities the vehicle possessed until the night she disappeared from outside of her mews. One of the men that took her was run over by the taxi, at the time Dmitri had assumed there was a driver, a partner, but when the only witness said there wasn't one he began to do some investigating into Verene, finding out that Tim was kitted out with all sorts of computer equipment, bullet proof windows and body work and many more attributes that gave him the powers to hunt down many criminals over the years in her service.

With Verene gone, he thought he would be able to get to her 'clients', two women who he understood to be relatives to the Romanovs but at first he had no idea how closely they were related, having tried unsuccessfully to get his hands on the taxi and then finding Verene's nephew had taken on the mantle of driving the black cab around he realised he was going to have to change tactics.

Over the years he kept a close eye on Jack and Tim until the day of the auction. The taxi driver was now a security guard at the auction house, but Dmitri also knew he was working for MI5 just like his aunt.

With Verene's connection to the two women and now Jack's many job titles and the fact he was guarding a Romanov egg Dmitri put two and two together and got one hell of a set of bells going off in his head.

This was when he saw the opportunity of getting hold of the bear until Antonio Strekotin got to it first, this was actually to his advantage as the auction brought the two mysterious women out into the open, he knew then his time of victory was close.

After calling in a lot of favours, which were more like threats he found that the two women had been living in hiding for years at Kensington Palace, with their likeness to the Romanovs although they tried to hide the fact and their connection to Vereene he knew he had found who he had spent years looking for, his mother and grandfather would be proud.

Now he was so close to getting his bloody revenge, at the same time starting a political war. He had heard rumours that all the files the Tsar had smuggled out of their mother country still existed but where and with whom was still a mystery, he had to take the risk when he ignited his war on the government and the Romanovs they would be revealed, it may be to his disadvantage but his revenge had taken such a hold on his insane mind it was a risk he was willing to take.

If it meant he would die, to him he would die a hero, a hero of the Old Revolution, Rasputin would finally win even in death, in his grandson's death.

He stood then walked slowly towards the exit, towards the light of a new day, a new political war……the warm sun engulfed him as he raised his arms into the air as if the rays filled him with more power.

With his long dark hair and mad eyes he was the image of his grandfather more than ever!

# CHAPTER THIRTY

Alex sat staring at his father as he slept in his chair, he looked so peaceful, the stress of the last few days barely showed on his resting features, just a little more pale than usual. Tim had dropped him off home after driving around for a while talking to him about his grandfather's history and connection with the bear. He was finding it near impossible to take it all in, but on the other hand he slowly began to realise all the clues had been there for years he just never picked up on them.

The poor man was still relatively in the dark about why his father was so obsessed with the bear and its former owner who ever they were. Tim realised that Antonio still knew more than he was letting on even to his own son, was that for his own safety or lack of trust? Tim hoped it was the former and himself kept a lot of the information private until he felt sure the time was right to fill Alex in completely.

As he watched the middle aged man slouch into the house he scanned the surrounding area for any lingering Russians. When he was sure it was safe he left for MI5 headquarters, but not until at least ten men were stationed around the house and surrounding area for Antonio and Alex's safety although the two of them were unaware of the protection.

Tim drove away slowly, just in case he saw anyone hiding in the shadows. Sure enough he saw something that he actually didn't expect.... a large lion sat licking it's lips as if waiting to pounce on its next prey.

Why would a lone lion be free in this concrete jungle? It was then that Tim saw someone hiding in the shadows behind the great beast.

Dmitri Rasputin, his dark eyes seemed to glow in the dim reflection of the street light, surrounding him in a yellow hue as if he was an apparition of pure evil. He smiled as he stared at the house, the lion moved forward, Dmitri placed a halting hand on the animal's head.

"Tim calling all protection, large lion sighted near the private park south entrance also sighted Dmitri Rasputin. Be alert that either could attack any moment please take precautions against animal attack." He also called it into MI5 headquarters, within seconds Jack was on the radio.

"Dear God, he's on the loose with one of his lions, well he should be easy to find even avoid!! Are Alex and Antonio safe?" Radio silence.

"Tim, Tim come in Tim." Jack couldn't understand why he wasn't answering, it was unlike him.

"Chief I'm off out." Jack didn't even bother waiting for an acknowledgement, although he could vaguely hear Gibson shouting after him..... "Jack what the hell is going on now, Jack, Jack oh dear God here we go again. Station one open the security doors ASAP for Agent Jack Courage and tell him to go careful." Exasperated the Chief dropped into his seat with his head dropping into his hands, he sometimes wondered how he didn't have a nervous breakdown thanks to Jack although he was his best agent he never went by the book.....ever!!!

Jack literally ran out of the garage into the darkened road and straight into the path of a black cab, luckily it stopped, of course it stopped, it was Tim coming to get him.

"You must have read my mind." Jack laughed at his friend and partner.

"Not too difficult really haha." Tim laughed as Jack got into the driving seat and they drove off back to Antonio's house. With so little traffic at such a late hour it didn't take long.

They didn't expect the sight that greeted them, every man Tim had posted around the area was dead, mauled to death by the lion.

Jack jumped out of Tim and ran towards the closest body, the poor man was still alive, he cradled him in his lap trying to stem the blood flow seeping from a stomach wound. The young man grabbed Jack's hand.....

"Dmitri, lion, couldn't stop them." The last bit of life in him left for the final time, his head lolled to the side as Jack bowed his in respect.

"Jack ruuuuuunnnnnnn!!!" Tim shouted across the square as he realised a large lion was bounding towards his friend. Jack in turn got up as quickly as possible and started running towards the protection of the taxi stopping abruptly as he realised his path to safety was blocked by a tall long haired man, his head cast down dark pinhead eyes gazing up at him with menace in his expression, his black lank hair hung framing his gaunt features.

Jack looked behind him to see the lion stood waiting, the man in front of him lifted his right arm in his hand an old pistol, he thought to himself as he gazed down the barrel if it was possible that it was so old it might not work. BANG!!! It worked! Only Jack felt no pain, just a whistling sound passing his left ear, followed by a haunting laughter as Dmitri found enjoyment in his uncertainty of what would happen next.

There was a thud behind Jack as the bullet had hit the lion wounding him enough to stop him, Dmitri realising his mistake screamed in anger and horror at hurting his own lion, he smashed the butt of the gun against Tim's body work in angry reaction.

"DO YOU MIND?!" Tim revved his engine and opened the back door hitting Dmitri so hard on his back he was thrown forward with such force he didn't have time to stop himself hitting the concrete road with such a thud he was winded and struggling to breath, his hands bled from the fall.

Jack saw this as his opportunity and grabbed the mad man's bleeding hands at the same time handcuffing them behind his back while he started to struggle as his breathing improved. Too late, he lay like a fish out of water flapping to get up.

Grabbing him by the scruff of his neck Jack literally dragged the man across the rough concrete of the road not taking any notice of his screams of agony even less so when he threw him into the back of Tim with a hell of a thud.

"I'll be back." Jack shut the door not even waiting to listen to see if the locking mechanism kicked in, he trusted Tim to do his bit. Walking towards the house he tutted sympathetically at each body he passed, such a waste. Then he came to the lion, in a split second the animal was up and lunged for him but dropped like a stone, dead to the floor, Jack looked open mouthed from the dead animal to Tim where a smoking barrel could be seen sticking out of his undercarriage.

"Bullseye"

"Or rather lion's eye, thanks Tim." Jack relaxed momentarily, caught his breath then carried on to the house.

As he reached the front door he realised it was open slightly, had the lion been in or Dmitri. He really hoped it wasn't a blood bath like outside.

He pushed the door slowly, it creaked loudly, darkness greeted him as did Alex. He stood frozen with fear holding onto the bannister for support, relaxing slightly as he saw it was Jack coming in.

"Thank God it's you, dear God what the hell was that, that was a lion?"

"Come on Alex, sit down, where's your father, is he ok?" Jack guided him to the front room where he was glad to see Antonio sat wide awake in his chair, he struggled to get up and greet Jack who in turn motioned for him to stay seated, at the same time helping Alex into another seat opposite his father.

"I'm afraid we will have to take you both into protective custody now for your own safety, just while we tie up a few loose ends. We also need to talk about the bear and all involved."

"There's no one else alive to be involved Mr Courage, no one." Antonio closed his eyes as a single tear slid down.

"Antonio I have some news for you which I think is going to be hard to take in. Alex I think you should get your father a strong drink….he's going to need it."

"The two women you saw at the auction are the daughter and granddaughter of Anastasia Romanov, your father's first love, the golden bear actually saved her life."

Antonio gasped as Jack mentioned the women.

"I knew there was something about them when they spoke to me, oh my dear father can now rest in peace. She lived, she lived a life. Now I understand her warning to me that day, she knew the Russians would come after the bear and myself" He smiled more to himself than anyone else, a look of peace spread over his old face at the thought of Anastassia surviving.

As Jack was explaining everything to him Tim radioed through to say that Dmitri was beginning to get agitated in the back of him and it was probably best they took him to The Chief at headquarters.

Tim had contacted a fellow black cab for Antonio and Alex's journey to MI5 there was no way they could travel in the back of him with Dmitri Rasputin.

It took less than half an hour to get to headquarters as the roads were still quiet at such an ungodly hour. Just before they headed off a team of 'clean up' guys had arrived to take care of the bodies and make it look like nothing had happened after photographs and evidence had been collected.

On arriving at headquarters Dmitri was literally dragged out of Tim, he didn't warrant being handled with kid gloves, this was a killer of many and a man that wanted to start a world war. His dark lank greasy hair barely hiding the eyes of a mad man as they stared at Jack. Dmitri smiled a knowing smile as if he knew of some impending doom that would befall Jack.

Jack in turn pushed him hard towards the door leading to the upstairs offices where the Chief would be waiting for them, he turned to face them as Dmitri fell through the door thanks to another shove by Jack.

Dmitri managed to stay standing, hands still cuffed behind his back. He flicked his hair off of his face then spat out a few words of warning.

"You cannot hold me here, I have diplomatic immunity." Laughing he struggled with his hands as if he could escape.

"No one knows you're here, no one to complain to, and do you really think I would let you go, the fact that you have killed so many innocent men and women over the years and planned to start a third world war, no Dmitri diplomatic immunity or not you are staying right here. Take him down to the cells......and throw away the key." The last few words were more to himself and wishful thinking.

Jack pushed him out of the office again and grabbing his arm with the help of two men. He took him down into another basement below the garage where......no one would hear you scream!!!!

# CHAPTER THIRTY ONE

"Your Highness it's time that the files are made public." The Prince's advisor stood behind him as he gazed out over the gardens of Kensington Palace. He had dreaded this day, he was well known for making the headlines himself but his involvement in this would make for more than headlines!!

"I suppose you're right Jenkins, I suppose you are right." He felt impending doom hanging in the air. To be honest he never really thought this day would ever come. Being left the responsibility of such information was a cross to bear in itself, if certain individuals got hold of any of the files all hell could break loose, the certainty of a third world war starting was too much of a risk to take. His main worry however was the history changing facts that were likely to come out, either way the Russian government is going to be damaged beyond repair and history books will have to be rewritten.

"Sir the files are here, where shall I have them laid out?" Jenkins stood back to let three men walk in carrying dirty looking file boxes he indicated for them to be placed on the large dining table, he touched them soon realising with disgust that they were covered in years of dust. He turned to the aged Prince who had now joined him by the table.

"Well let's get started, have you liaised with our MI5 contact?"

Jenkins shifted uncomfortably, "I'm afraid she is no longer with us Sir, but my contacts have informed me that her nephew has taken over her mantle and is involved in the situation all be it none the wiser as to how much is at stake."

"I suggest you contact him as soon as possible, Jenkins and get him here."

The Prince lifted the lid off of box 1, he sighed at the sight that greeted him, a tatty picture of his long lost relative Tsar Nicholas, such a sad sad loss. If only our men had got to him in time.

Prince Philip sat down and began to go through the first box. The files covered in years of dust, and full of information against the Russian government, naming every man who had been involved in meetings to bring down the Romanov family and the written evidence of the lies that were told to irreversibly blacken their names to the extent that their own people and country wanted them dead.

Information on who was blackmailing who and why, always to gain power over the country and make money. Lists of people who were tortured, why and by whom and for what political gain.

So many high powered people involved the Romanovs didn't stand a chance.

He sat for hours reading and rereading until he came to the last file, it was thinner than all the others. He read that King George V had been in talks with Tsar Nicholas regarding getting him and his family out of the country before the revolution could take hold, the King had sent some of his best men to get them out of their palace. When they had arrived they found that the Tsar and his family had been imprisoned in the Ipatiev house. They managed to get a small secret army together making their way to the large house only to find carnage, the family slaine and buried in a shallow grave in the grounds.

The King was told as soon as possible and was said to have broken down at the news which was a shock to all around as he was regarded as a hard emotionless man, but this was his cousin, his family.

The world was under the impression that the King had stabbed the Tsar in the back by not giving them asylum, he could not reveal the fact that his men were going in undercover or that they were too late and he certainly couldn't reveal the survival of Anastasia, as even they didn't know at first because they mistakenly thought the body of a maid was the Princess. It wasn't until sometime later that they realised the possibility of her survival was more likely.

After his secret army did some investigating they managed to find her and help her escape to Paris where King George took responsibility of protecting her via allies in the French government whom he could trust with the secret of her survival.

His people say he was never the same again, the one ray of light in his life was the secret survival of Anastasia and thankfully he lived long enough to see her once again in a secret meeting in Paris, he found her happily married to Louis Bonaparte and gifted them all the protection they needed but when Louis was brutally murdered he insisted on her and her daughter and granddaughter moving to London and the safety of Kensington Palace.

The Palace was filled with old and new members of the Royal Family, some even the public thought had died years ago! It was like a Royal commune, full of tradition, maids and butlers old and young. Some members of the family had not left the confines of the palace for so long they wouldn't recognise the outside world.

The only modern day effect was the security, bullet and torpedo proof glass windows for starters. No one not even the best of the best would get into the Palace.

The King died knowing they were finally safe, he died knowing he had let his cousin and the rest of the family down. He died a guilty broken man.

Prince Philip, a hard navel man, a stubborn man cried for the innocent that had died, for the return of a small tatty bear to a young girl who never stopped running for her life.

# CHAPTER THIRTY TWO

"Sir Mr Courage." Jenkins backed out of the room bowing.

Jack just stood there to attention, he bowed his head in respect when the Prince reaslised he had entered the room and approached him. Jack had no idea why he was here but had an inclin that it had something to do with Anastasia. He noticed in the background the files covering the antique table, he also noticed the Prince's hands were dirty, he had obviously been handling the mountain of paperwork.

The Prince turned expecting Jack to follow him to the table, he fiddled with the edges of a file deep in thought trying to find the words and where to start.

"Sir, I know Anastasia survived, we have her daughter, granddaughter and a maid in protective custody, I know they have been living here in the confines of the Palace, right under our noses. I'm sorry about Anastasia and her family."

It was a while until either man spoke, both stood staring down at the files. So much history, so much bloodshed and all here on paper, like a thriller novel. Only this wasn't a story, this was a truth waiting to be told.

There were piles of files full of unreputiple evidence against the Russian government but one man in particular who was in custody right now had his own file which was the thickest.....the grandson of Rasputin, Dmitri.

"These files will change the history books, it may or may not start another cold war I have no idea anymore but so many innocent people have died because of greed, of the financial and political kind. Do you have the bear with you?"

Jack was thrown by the throwaway request, why would the Prince want the bear? As it happened he had brought it with him, for some reason he felt he had to but couldn't think why. Without taking his eyes off of the Prince he took the bear out of his rucksack and was about to hand it to the Prince but the old man just walked out of the room, again expecting Jack to follow.

They exchanged looks as they left the room and then a very shiny old Russian penny began to drop.

The look on the Prince's face told him something he never thought possible, the sadness and relief at the same time in his eyes spoke volumes.

"Oh my God you can't mean........." Jack didn't get chance to finish his sentence as the Prince led him up some stairs along one of the many dark corridors of the palace, if only the walls of this place could talk.

The once handsome Prince now almost 100 himself walked slowly, his retirement from public duty had not been due to health matters but to carry on his search for the 'Truth' as to what happened to Anastasia and her family. He came to the end of a long corridor.

There was a nurse sitting at an antique desk outside a room, the only sound were the birds singing outside and the ticking of ancient clocks. The Prince nodded at the old lady as she slowly stood and curtsied. She walked to the door gently opening it to reveal in the dimly lit room the silhouette of an old woman lay in a hospital bed in front of a window. In the beam of sunlight that slipped in through a large crack in the heavy curtains fragments of dust danced like angels watching over her.

Prince Philip stood back for Jack to enter, for a moment he stood frozen to the spot clutching the bear tightly, his grip tightened as he caught sight of the old bedridden woman.

Looking from the bear to the woman who lay motionless, her shallow breathing almost inaudible.

"Anastasia.....er I have something for you......it's your teddy bear that Alexander Strekotin gave you."

Jack took a step back as she gasped in recognition of what he said, her aged eyes shot open, her old bony hand rose towards him, slowly stepping towards her he placed the tatty bear in it. She let out a heavy sigh as she clasped it to her chest as she whispered "Okh moya lyubov" 'Oh my love'.

"This bear saved my life you know." A longing smile crept over her face almost bare of wrinkles, she held the bear to her chest as she turned to look at Jack with tears in her eyes...

"Blagodaryu vas" 'Thank you'

"I didn't understand how the bear could have saved you Ma'am, but now I do"

"The bullet meant for my heart." She pointed to the golden belly button. A cheeky smile warmed her face, a wink that made Jack smile. The belly button was the missing bullet, stopped by the old stuffing inside the toy, no wonder the Russians were desperate to get their hands on him.

She slowly turned her head on the pillow to look at the bear then the stunning sunrise, the curtains now fully open to reveal more of the sunlight as it hit the belly button filling the room with a warm glow......she sighed......she could rest now, she could join her Alexander, as the sun rose her grip on the bear loosened, a quiet sigh left her lips as Anastasia quietly passed away, now at peace.....now she could stop running.

Jack turned to find Ana and Alexandria stood in the doorway, tears streaming down their faces.

"Thank you for finding my mother peace, thank you."

Prince Philip wiped away a tear, straightened his shoulders, bowed his head and retreated leaving the women to grieve once more but for one final time.

Somewhere deep within the cold cemented confines of MI5's headquarters a mad man clutched at his heart as if the hand of God himself was ripping it out of his chest, Dmitri knew then that his grandfather had lost once more to the Romanovs, he sensed the death of a beautiful young girl, Dmitri's psychic powers were sometimes a painful hindrance, a reminder of his and his families failings.

He let out a ferrall wolf like howl, a roar like a lion then dropped dead as his heart gave out, divine intervention? No one knew, he lay face down arms outstretched like he had been crucified............no one mourned.

Darkness can hide many secrets, horrors even the strongest man could not handle. but some secrets fight to be told, to find justice for the victims unable to defend themselves, no matter how many years have passed.

Silhouetted against the night sky lit only by the ghost-like moon stood the cold stone skeleton of a large ruin.

Although crumbling it stood proud like a lion waiting to pounce on its next prey.

The darkness of its windows like eyes to its soul, the blackened doorway, the devil's own gateway to hell.

A heavy door slams, he turns startled, the dust lingers in the air, panic rushing through his body. Turning round and around, the sound of girls laughing and soldiers barking out orders, gunshots, silence.

Just the sound of his blood rushing through his head and his own heavy laboured breathing.

The air thick with dust, gun smoke and the smell of fresh blood. He gagged, his hand slapped against his mouth.

No birds have sung in the grounds since 1918, only the bravest or stupidest people scramble through the broken down masonry and rusted barbed wire fences once erected to keep them out, if only for their own sanity.

Alexander turned away from the ruin as Anastasia ran towards him, his arms outstretched for the love he never stopped searching for, the sun shone brighter today than it ever had or ever would again as the two young lovers were reunited once more for eternity. The ruin of Ipatiev House slowly vanished leaving fields of green surrounding the young couple, he kissed her gently as a small golden teddy bear slowly dropped to the ground as they embraced once more, never to be parted again.

True love always wins........ to live to the beat of the hearts that are true to each other, always.

The end..........? it's only the beginning.....

Lightning Source UK Ltd.
Milton Keynes UK
UKHW010631100621
385271UK00001B/176